WILLIAM AND THE
BRAINS TRUST

By the Same Author

"YOU GO ROUND AND FIND OUT WHICH IS OURS AND
WHICH IS THE ENEMY," SAID WILLIAM.

(See page 59.)

WILLIAM AND THE BRAINS TRUST

BY
RICHMAL CROMPTON

ILLUSTRATED BY
THOMAS HENRY

LONDON
GEORGE NEWNES LIMITED
TOWER HOUSE, SOUTHAMPTON STREET
STRAND, W.C.2

First Published . . . 1945
Second Impression . . . 1945
Third Impression . . . 1948
Fourth Impression . . . 1950
Fifth Impression . . . 1952

Printed in Great Britain by
Wyman & Sons, Limited, London, Fakenham and Reading

CONTENTS

CHAPTER I

WILLIAM AND THE BRAINS TRUST

IT was the time when the Brains Trust movement, so rashly started by the B.B.C., was sweeping England. Every town, every village, every parish, every street had its Brains Trust, at whose meetings earnest seekers after knowledge discussed the scientific, political or economic problems of the day. The more enterprising ones induced eminent authorities on these subjects to visit and address them—a process which, generally speaking, added to their public prestige and to their private bewilderment.

The village in which William lived was not immune from this latest craze. A local Brains Trust, under the direction of Mr. Markson, the head master of the school which William attended and the acknowledged intellectual leader of the neighbourhood, met regularly at the various members' houses and discussed such things as the Theory of Time, the Beveridge Report, Post-War Reconstruction and the Origin of Matter. A mild sensation was caused when it was announced that the Vicar had secured the attendance of Professor Knowle at their next meeting. Professor Knowle was one of the originators of the Brains Trust idea and took part regularly in Radio Brains Trust discussions. He had been at college with the Vicar, and, though they had not met since, he remembered him, or said he remembered him, quite well—well enough to make him break his rule of never speaking outside London except to university audiences. The news spread rapidly, and so many people wished to attend the meeting that the Brains Trust decided to hire the Church Room at Marleigh in order to accommodate them.

William was not particularly interested in all this. He had listened once to the B.B.C. Brains Trust on the wireless and had been so bored that he had taken care never to listen again. Moreover, he had other interests at present. The airmen attached to Marleigh aerodrome, who were billeted in or near Marleigh, were getting up a variety show to be held in Marleigh Village Hall in aid of the R.A.F. Benevolent Fund. There was to be a comic ballet, a comic pantomime, conjuring, and various skits on the personnel and routine of the aerodrome. William had made many friends among the airmen and took a lively interest in the proceedings. He had even been allowed to attend some of the rehearsals and to help with the curtain (which he generally pulled up or lowered at the wrong moment) and to carry on and off the various rudimentary stage properties required for the scenes. He had canvassed the countryside with tickets and had been gratified to find that as many tickets were sold for the R.A.F. show as for Mr. Markson's Brains Trust. It was unfortunate that both events were to take place on the same night. Professor Knowle was a man of many engagements, and that date was his only free evening for many months to come, while the various duties of the members of the concert party also made any other night impossible There were, however, sufficient local inhabitants to fill both the Church Room and the Village Hall, and all bought tickets. The high-brows bought tickets for the Brains Trust, and the low-brows for the concert party. In order to emphasise the lack of rivalry, the Vicar had invited the whole concert party to the Vicarage for refreshments after their show.

William had arranged to "help" with the dress rehearsal of the concert party. He was deeply proud of his position as curtain manipulator and scene shifter. He had even been allowed to prompt at the last rehearsal, and, though he had by mistake turned over two pages of the script together and thrown all the company out, he still felt that he carried the entire weight of responsibility for the proceedings on his own shoulders.

On the morning of the day of the dress rehearsal he walked into the Village Hall with an air of importance. No cheerful "Hello, nipper" greeted him. A few members of the cast stood about disconsolately. They turned lack-lustre eyes on him, as if hardly recognising him. He felt some disaster in the air, and his heart sank.

"Hello," he said tentatively.

They did not even answer him.

"What time are we goin' to start?" he said.

"Never, probably," said someone morosely.

It turned out that the "stars" of the concert party had been posted to a northern aerodrome preparatory to going overseas and had left early that morning. The concert party was shorn of its best comedian, its deepest bass, its conjurer, its tap dancer, its crooner. "Don't see how we can carry on at all," said a tall, thin corporal who sang "Sailing, Sailing," in front of the curtain while the conjurer was getting his "props" ready.

"Well, we can't back out of it now," said a short stout one who performed indifferently on the ukelele.

So the rehearsal continued—uninspired, grey, devoid of pep. They did their best. The man who sang "Sailing, Sailing," added "Drinking, Drinking," and "Watchman, What of the Night?" to his repertoire, the man who played the ukelele did a few transparent conjuring tricks, which, he said optimistically, would probably come off all right on the night, the pianist added a little thing of his own composition, and the second best comedian said that he'd try to get hold of a comic monologue that he remembered hearing somewhere or other some time or other . . . but on the whole the rehearsal was not a success.

William walked home slowly and sadly. He wished he were a famous comedian, a famous conjurer, a famous tap dancer, a famous crooner, so that he could rescue his heroes from their plight.

As he passed the gate of the Vicarage, he came upon the Vicar and Mr. Markson conversing together earnestly.

"One minute, Brown," said Mr. Markson, and went on talking to the Vicar. William hovered in the background.

"His train gets in at six-thirty," the Vicar was saying, "but he particularly doesn't want to be met. He'll go straight to the Church Room."

"It seems rather casual to let him make his way there alone," said Mr. Markson. "I could easily meet him."

"Oh, no, he's a very shy man," said the Vicar. "He hates fuss. Anything in the nature of an official reception would scare him so much that he'd go straight back home."

"Very well," smiled Mr. Markson. "He's certainly an attraction. I understand that every seat's booked."

"He's more than an attraction, my dear sir," said the Vicar. "He's an inspiration. He holds his audiences spellbound."

"Splendid!" said Mr. Markson, then he turned to William and entrusted him with a message to the school caretaker, and went on his way.

William walked towards the school—slowly and thoughtfully but no longer sadly. An idea had occurred to him. This Professor Knowle was, it seemed, an "attraction," an "inspiration." He "held his audiences spellbound." He was just what the concert party needed. . . . He would fill the gap left by the comedian, the bass, the conjurer, the tap dancer, the crooner. . . . It was unfair that such a prize should fall to the lot of mere civilians, when he could aid the war effort by lending pep to the R.A.F. concert party. William did not stop to consider whether Professor Knowle's performance would be suitable to the concert party. He was an "attraction," an "inspiration," he "held his audiences spellbound." Therefore the concert party must have him. . . . He realised that the Vicar and Mr. Markson might not appreciate this point of view, and that even the R.A.F. concert party might be troubled by scruples of con- science on the subject. Fortunately William himself was not troubled by scruples of conscience. The matter was quite simple in his eyes. Professor Knowle must appear as the star turn of the concert party, and he, William, must proceed at once to draw up a plan of campaign.

He delivered his message to the school caretaker with such absent-minded politeness that the caretaker, who was accustomed to full-scale hostilities in his dealings with William, gazed after him in a troubled fashion, wondering if he were sickening for something. . . .

The plan of campaign seemed fairly simple. Pro-

"I'LL TAKE YOU A SHORT CUT OVER THE FIELDS, IF YOU LIKE," SAID WILLIAM.

fessor Knowle was not being met at the station. He was to find his own way to Marleigh Church Room. He would probably ask his way from anyone who happened to be in the vicinity. There was no reason why William himself should not happen to be in the vicinity. The thought of the Brains Trust, bereft of the brightest jewel in its crown, did not worry him. They were all good at talking. The absence of one talker, however good, in such an assembly would probably make little difference.

Professor Knowle descended from the train at the little wayside station, much relieved to find no solemn reception committee awaiting him. It was a fine evening, and he was looking forward to a pleasant country walk before his lecture. He asked a porter the way to Marleigh, and set off briskly along the road. After a short distance he came upon a boy sitting on a gate, sharpening a stick with a pen-knife.

"Am I on the right road to Marleigh, my boy?" he asked.

"What part do you want to go to?" said the boy.

"The Church Room," said Professor Knowle.

"I'll take you a short cut over the fields, if you like," said the boy.

That, thought the Professor, would be very nice. It was a warm evening, and the fields looked delightfully cool and green.

Together they set off across the fields. The boy, the professor decided, was not very intelligent. He replied shortly to all the professor's questions and appeared to take no interest in any of the subjects of conversation introduced by the professor. It suggested

to the professor a possible subject for future discussion.
Is the Town Child more Mentally Alert than the Country
Child? Certainly this country child did not seem
mentally alert. His face wore a wooden, almost a
blank, expression, and he did not seem to take any
interest in anything. Bucolic, thought the professor.
Undeveloped. But perhaps he wasn't a fair specimen
of the country child. They couldn't all, surely, be
quite as stupid as this. . . .

The child led him to a large hall, entering by a door

that led into a small room behind the stage. For the
first time it occurred to William that perhaps he ought
to have warned his friends of the new star he was
introducing into their midst, but, curiously, they
showed no surprise. For, as it happened, the second
best comedian had written home telling his family of
the straits to which his concert party was reduced,
and his brother, who was a much better comedian
even than the one they had lost, and who happened

WHEN THE PROFESSOR APPEARED A WILD BURST OF
APPLAUSE AROSE.

to be spending seven days' leave at home, had sent a
wire: "Don't worry. Will come along and give you
a hand." The comedian knew that one of his brother's
best "turns" was "Professor Know-all" an imitation
of Professor Knowle of the B.B.C. Brains Trust, and,
therefore, he was not at all surprised to see the professor
entering the small door at the rear of the stage in the
Village Hall. He came in the nick of time, for they
had just reached the item described on the programme

as "Mystery Item." They had hoped that someone would have a brilliant idea for it at the last minute, but so far no one had any idea for it at all. . . .

The comedian, on catching sight of the professor, gave a yell of joy, smote him heartily on the back and said: "Splendid, old fellow, splendid! I knew you wouldn't let me down."

The professor was a little surprised by this unconventional greeting, but there was no time for discussion, as the comedian, with a "Go straight on, old boy. They're waiting for you," thrust him up a small flight of stairs on to the platform.

There again the professor found his reception somewhat disconcertingly hearty. The moment he appeared a wild burst of applause arose. His audience rocked and roared with laughter, stamped, clapped and shouted. "Marvellous" . . . "Wonderful" . . . "Might be the real one" . . . The fact that the real one was presumably addressing an audience only a few yards away added zest to the situation. The applause grew to deafening proportions and showed no signs of dying down. The laughter did not discompose the professor. It interested him. He was not accustomed to country audiences, and he had fully expected their reactions to be different from those of a town audience. They were pleased to see him, gratified at his coming, and their laughter was merely an expression of their feelings. "The loud laugh that speaks the empty mind." Bucolic, again. Like the boy who had brought him there.

After about five minutes the applause died down sufficiently to enable him to make his voice heard.

"Ladies and gentlemen," he said, "I am here to-night to speak to you on the Theory of Relativity . . ."

Another burst of wild applause rang out. The voice . . . the intonations . . . the little mannerisms (immortalised by a recent film) . . . all were so exactly true to life that, as the audience said over and over again in rapturous delight: "It's *marvellous* . . . it might be the real one."

Meantime the Vicar and Mr. Markson stood at the door of the Village Hall, anxiously consulting their watches.

"He must have missed the train," said the Vicar.

"I'm afraid so," said the head master.

"Of course it's just possible that he's not coming from London," said the Vicar. "His engagements take him all over the place. A train from Birmingham gets in shortly after the London one. He may be coming by that."

They waited a few more minutes . . . then suddenly espied a familiar figure making its way across the fields from the station. A thrill shot through both their hearts. There he was—the world-famous form, the embodiment of intellect, the pride of learning, the revered leader of every seeker after knowledge—reddish beard, projecting eyebrows, broad-brimmed hat and all—in their midst.

They crossed the field to meet him.

"Welcome, welcome, my dear sir," said the Vicar.

"Don't mention it, don't mention it, don't mention it," said the newcomer in the rather squeaky high-pitched voice that the wireless had made so familiar to them.

"You've come from Birmingham, I presume?" said Mr. Markson.

"Yes," squeaked the visitor. "I spent all this morning fishing from the end of the pier there."

They glanced at each other in slight bewilderment. A little deaf, probably, like most elderly professors. . . . But they had reached the Church Room now.

"NOW, FRIENDS," SAID PROFESSOR KNOW-ALL, "SHOOT
A FEW QUESTIONS AT ME."

"Would you like a rest first, sir," said the Vicar, "or will you go straight on?"

"If it's time for my turn, I'll go straight on," said the visitor.

An odd way of putting it, thought the Vicar, but most great men were a little eccentric.

The second best comedian's brother in his famous impersonation, "Professor Know-all" stepped on to the stage. The audience applauded loudly. He looked round. . . . Queer-looking lot of buffers . . . Not the sort of audience he was used to . . . Pity he hadn't seen his brother first and got a bit of dope on what was expected of him, but he supposed his brother and the other chaps were busy in a green room

of some sort somewhere, and this padre—or someone dressed up as a padre—was compèring. Yes, he was making a speech now, introducing him. Jolly good take-off of the sort of speech padres make introducing people, too. It made him chuckle several times. No one in the audience laughed, but country audiences were always a bit heavy on hand. It took a lot to make them laugh, but that didn't mean they weren't amused. The compère, still doing a jolly good take-off of a padre, was calling on him to speak.

"Jolly good, old chap," he murmured as he rose to his feet. "Excellent."

He stood for a few moments, waiting for the applause to die down, doing a few of his more famous imitations of the professor's mannerisms—stroking his beard, passing his hand over his head, screwing up his eyes . . .

"Now, friends," he said, "shoot a few questions at me, and I'll do my best to answer them."

He always found that a good way of beginning. They asked crazy questions, and he gave crazy answers.

A woman got up and began to talk about Relativity. It was a jolly good take-off of the way people carried on at these Brains Trust meetings, but, though they all listened with obvious appreciation, no one laughed. Certainly, it took a lot to get 'em going in this part of the world. And she went on too long. Didn't seem to know that the main point of guying anyone is to know when to stop. Professor Know-all had had a tiring journey and had been up late at a very good party the night before. His eyelids dropped . . . He awoke from his doze—partially, at any rate— several times, but someone was always talking— either the first woman, or another very like her or a

man very like both. The "turn" didn't seem to
need him any longer. Actually, of course, he'd done
his bit. . . . All he had to do on these occasions was
to get himself up as Professor Know-all, bring out
the voice and mannerisms, and after that the thing
went with a swing by itself.

Someone was doing a jolly good take-off of a vote
of thanks now, talking about the "inspiration of his
presence" and a lot more comic stuff like that, but
still no one laughed. Odd, but then people in the
country *were* odd. . . . The compère was talking
about him now. Still pretty good, but, like the woman,
he didn't seem to realise that you could overdo a
"take-off" . . . There was a note of apology in the
Vicar's speech. He realised that the members of the
Brains Trust had been so intent on "showing off"
before the great man that they had left the great
man nothing to do himself. Still, the Vicar felt that
the Brains Trust—inspired by the giant of intellect,
sitting there so still he might have been asleep, his
eyes cast down in thought as he weighed the arguments
of the various speakers—had acquitted itself well,
had risen to heights it had never reached in any of
its previous discussions, had proved that the torch of
knowledge was alight even in this little out-of-the-way
village. The professor must surely be impressed by the
results of his influence, by the far-reaching effects of the
movement he had started.

Professor Know-all found himself being led out of
the Church Room and across the fields to the Vicarage.
Two of the women who had done most of the talking
during his "turn", accompanied him, still talking. He
began to feel a little bewildered. He hadn't seen his

brother or any of the other performers. He hadn't seen any other "turn" but his own. His own had certainly gone off quite well, and the audience had risen to the joke splendidly, but—there was something about the whole thing he couldn't quite understand.

"Can you explain the Infinite Regress Theory of Time, Professor?" said one of the women earnestly.

"Sure, sister," said the pseudo professor easily. "There's not much old Know-all can't explain, but let's give the thing a break for a bit. We've all had about enough of it. . . . Have you had Ensa down here lately? . . . There's a chap there who can take off Bernard Shaw so you wouldn't know the difference."

"Really?" said the seeker after knowledge politely.

Professor Knowle accompanied the rest of the concert party across the fields to the Vicarage. The whole thing had been a bit bewildering. Despite the laughter that had punctuated his speech, there had been no doubt of its success, for the applause at the end had been terrific. When he invited questions, a man in R.A.F. uniform had asked "Where do the flies go in the winter time?" and another "What makes the fizz in champagne?" and the professor had tried conscientiously to answer both. Frenzied burst of applause had greeted both questions and answers.

Then a man had come from behind the stage, clapped him on the back till he was sore and said: "It was great, old chap. Simply great. Now go and sit down in front and see the rest of the show."

So the professor sat down in front and saw the rest of the show. Evidently the local Brains Trust was testifying its gratitude to him for his visit by getting up a sort of entertainment in his honour. An original and rather touching idea. . . . It suggested a subject for discussion. Is there More Originality in a Country Community than in a Town Community? He had been to innumerable Brains Trust discussions and never come across anything like this before. The entertainment itself was a little difficult to follow, but the audience enjoyed it, laughing uproariously—their usual way, apparently, of expressing appreciation. . . .

And now it was over, and he was being escorted across the field by a crowd of men, mostly in uniform, who kept hitting him on the back and saying: "You were great, old chap. Simply great" . . . "Went like a rocket from beginning to end" . . . "You're a real sport to come over and get us out of a hole like this." . . . "Screaming, old chap! Screaming!" . . . "Wizard!" . . . "Star turn. . . ."

Surrounded by this bewildering crowd of large enthusiastic men, he was shepherded up the Vicarage drive and into the drawing-room. And there, in front of the fireplace, the centre of a little circle of men and women who were still discoursing on Relativity and the Infinite Regress Theory of Time, stood Professor Know-all. The Vicar looked from one to the other and his face flushed darkly. He crossed the room to the newcomer and said sternly: "This, sir, is in extremely bad taste."

Professor Knowle gaped at him. The moment was, without doubt, the climax of the strangest evening he had ever spent in his life. "I beg your pardon?" he said dazedly.

"Extremely bad taste," repeated the Vicar with increasing severity. "A joke ceases to be a joke when

"THIS IS IN EXTREMELY BAD TASTE," SAID THE VICAR.

it oversteps the bounds of propriety.   This is an insult
to my guest, sir."

With that he returned to Professor Know-all, who
was looking even more bewildered than his model.

"I hope you will pardon this ill-timed impersonation,
sir," he said.   "The man means no harm, I assure
you."

At that moment the comedian entered.   He bounded
across the room, brushed the vicar and the earnest

seekers after knowledge aside, smote the pseudo
professor heartily on the back, pulled his beard,
tweaked his eyebrows, cuffed his head, and said:

"You were grand, old chap. Simply grand. You
brought the house down!"

"My dear sir!" expostulated the Vicar faintly.

Everyone looked at everyone else in a dazed kind
of way, except the two brothers, who continued to
shake each other's hands and roar with laughter,
wholly oblivious to the amazement and bewilderment
around them.

It was the professor who took charge of the situation.
He stepped resolutely up to his double and said:
"Look here, who are we? Let's get it clear."

With a certain amount of difficulty they got it clear.

"It was the boy's mistake, of course," said the
professor, "and quite an understandable one. I
suppose that to a child—and rather a stupid child—
the Church Room and Village Hall are very much
alike."

"Did he say what his name was?" said Mr. Markson.

"He said it was William Brown. He's not to be
blamed, of course. He couldn't know what complications would ensue. . . ."

"I wonder . . ." said the head master thoughtfully.

But it was no use wondering. He could imagine
the wooden blankness of William's expression as he
persisted that he had misunderstood the professor and
thought that he meant the Village Hall. Better leave
the matter as it was. Besides, the two professors were
getting on together excellently—both laughing heartily
at the joke. He'd have liked an explanation with
the young rascal, but—better leave the matter as it was.

CHAPTER II

MRS. BOTT'S BIRTHDAY PRESENT

VIOLET ELIZABETH BOTT was of a contrary disposition. In peace-time she had frequently ignored her mother's birthday altogether. At best, she had given little time or thought or money to it, going down to the village at the last minute to buy something that she wanted herself, in the hope that Mrs. Bott would see no alternative but to give it back to her. This year, however, although it was war-time and Violet Elizabeth had every excuse to limit her attentions to an expression of goodwill, she chose to "make a nuisance of herself," as William put it, pestering him continually for suggestions and rejecting every one he made.

"No, I *can't* give her thweeth, William," she said, her habitual lisp accentuated by indignation at the suggestion. "I can hardly get enough for mythelf. Bethideth, thee mightn't give me them back if I did, cauth ith war-time and thee liketh thweeth herthelf."

"Give her a handkerchief."

"You can't, cauth of couponth."

"Give her an ornament."

"Thee'th got enough. Thee juth thendth them to jumble thaleth."

"Oh, well, I don't care. I'm sick of your ole mother's birthday, anyway. There's a war on. Don't give her anything."

"I mutht give her thomething," said Violet Elizabeth virtuously. "Thee'th my mother."

"I never said she wasn't," said William. "Anyway, that's no reason for givin' people presents in war-time."

"Yeth, it ith, William," persisted Violet Elizabeth.

"Well, anyway, it's nothin' to do with me," said William. "I'm busy, an' I'm not goin' to bother with it any more."

For William had formed a new and exciting friendship with a real army sergeant. He was not the burly army sergeant of tradition. He was a small, worried-looking man, with an anxious expression and a deprecating manner.

William, hotly pursuing an imaginary band of routed enemies round a corner of the road one afternoon, had run into the sergeant and sent him rolling in the dust. He was on the point of taking to flight in his turn, when he saw to his surprise that the sergeant, rising to his feet and brushing the dust from his knees, was smiling.

"Now, who were you chargin' like that, young fellow-me-lad? Was it Red Indians, by any chance?"

William gasped. It *had* been Red Indians.

"Used to chase 'em myself," chuckled the sergeant. "For miles an' miles. Never put up much of a fight, mine didn't."

"Mine jolly well did," said William emphatically. "I killed *dozens* of 'em before they took to flight."

"Oh, I used to kill dozens of 'em, too," said the sergeant.

It turned out that the sergeant and William had many tastes in common. The sergeant, like William, was at home in the countryside and woods. His

B

father had been a gamekeeper, and his knowledge of wood lore surpassed even William's.

"I say! You'll come in the woods with me one day, will you?" said William.

The sergeant's face clouded over.

"Come into the woods!" he echoed bitterly. "I don't get no time to go nowhere. We're here on a Course, you know. Special Course. I won't tell you *what* Course, 'case Hitler's listening. But that's all right. I don't mind the Course an' I don't mind the lads. It's '*im*!'"

"Who?" asked William.

The little sergeant screwed up his face into an expression of deep distaste.

"Capting Fuss-pot. 'E's in charge of us. A little 'ound, that's wot 'e is, though I didn't oughter say so. Fuss, fuss, fuss! Nag, nag, nag! An' it all comes on me. I don't mind work. I never 'ave. But 'is fuss gets me down. Can't tell you what to do an' leave you to do it. 'As to come fussin' round you all the time you're a-doin' of it. Gets on yer nerves. Fuss, fuss, fuss! Nag, nag, nag! An' time orf?" He laughed a hollow laugh. "''E's got to give the lads a bit of time orf, but me? Oh, no. When I'm not doin' 'is typin' I'm runnin' 'is messages for 'im. Mr. Bloomin' Fuss-pot!"

William saw the Captain in the village the next day—a short stout pompous-looking young man, with sleek dark hair and a high colour. He strutted importantly along in the middle of the road, throwing contemptuous glances around him. It was evident that he cherished no small opinion of himself.

The soldiers were encamped in one of Farmer Jenks'

fields, and occasionally William would stand at the hedge to watch them drilling, the Captain engaged in his favourite pastime of Throwing his Weight About, and the little sergeant scurrying busily here and there, trying to placate him. Sometimes the sergeant would find time for a few words with William over the hedge.

"'E's somethink *orful* to-day," he would groan. "Snap, snap, snap! Nag, nag, nag! Fuss, fuss, fuss! 'E's givin' no one no peace. Me especially. Don't think I'll ever 'ave time for that walk in the woods with you. I've gotter do all 'is typin' for 'im soon as I'm orf duty."

So the question of Mrs. Bott's birthday present seemed a trivial and unimportant one to William, and it irritated him that Violet Elizabeth seemed to consider that he shared the responsibility equally with her.

"Haven't you thought of thomething *yet*?" she would ask him sternly.

"Gosh, no! Why should I?" William would retort indignantly.

"Well, why thouldn't you?" retorted Violet Elizabeth with equal indignation.

So persistent was she that William, to his own annoyance, began to feel a certain responsibility for Mrs. Bott's birthday present.

"Can't you get her a—a necklace or something?" he suggested vaguely.

"Don't be thilly," snapped Violet Elizabeth. "Thee's got thouthandth of necklatheth."

"Well . . . a milk jug or something."

"Thath thillier thtill," said Violet Elizabeth. "There ithn't enough milk for the oneth we've got."

"Well, I can't think of anything else," said William. "I'm just about sick of it, an', anyway, it isn't my business."

"Oh, William, *pleathe*! An' it'th to-morrow. You *mutht* think of thomething."

"Well, I can't. I've told you I can't."

"Come back to tea, William, an' we can think together." She saw a refusal trembling on William's

"I'VE NEVER WALKED, NOT SINCE BOTTY MADE 'IS
PILE," SAID MRS. BOTT, ANGRILY.

lips and hastened to add: "There'th chocolate
bithcuith."

The refusal ceased to tremble on William's lips.

"All right, I'll come," he said, adding ungraciously,
"if you're *sure* there's chocolate biscuits."

"Yeth, there ith," Violet Elizabeth assured him.
"Honethtly, there ith."

William accompanied her up the drive of the Hall and in at the big front door.

"Now I've not promised to *think* of anything," he stipulated, as he wiped his feet on the mat. "I've only come 'cause there's chocolate biscuits."

"Yeth, William," agreed Violet Elizabeth meekly. "but p'rapth thomething will *come* to you while you're eating them."

Mrs. Bott was entertaining a visitor and bemoaning the harshness and tyranny of the Government in forbidding her the use of her car. Wife of Mr. Bott, of Bott's Sauces, she was the local Lady of the Manor. She was generous, impulsive, incalculable, short-tempered and irredeemably common—a thorn in the side of her more aristocratic neighbours. What she lacked in refinement, however, she made up in forcefulness of character.

"'Ow do they think I'm goin' to get about?" she demanded.

"I suppose they think we can walk," suggested the visitor mildly.

Violet Elizabeth neatly abstracted the dish of chocolate biscuits from the cake stand, and put it on the window seat between William and herself.

"Eat ath many ath you like, William," she whispered, "and p'rapth thomething will *come* to you."

William, without waiting for any further encouragement, set to work. . . .

Mrs. Bott threw them an absent glance and continued her lamentations.

"Walk!" she repeated bitterly. "I never 'ave walked—not since Botty made 'is pile. Wot's the

good of Botty 'avin' made all that money, if I've got to
start walkin' at my age? *Walkin'*. *Me!*"

"What about a bicycle?" ventured the visitor.

"A *what*? I wouldn't be seen on one of them
things, not if I was paid for it. I couldn't balance on
it, to start with—not with my figure. Now I shouldn't
mind a carriage. There's somethin' classy about a
carriage. But you can't get 'em. An' there ain't no
'orses, neither. I wouldn't mind even a nanny goat.
I used to wish I 'ad a nanny goat cart when I was a
child. I bet I could ride in one even now. I'm not
as 'eavy as what I look, an' they're stronger than what
they look, are nanny goats. But you can't get them,
neither."

"Oh, well," said the visitor, trying to introduce a
more cheerful note, "I suppose it will all be over one
of these days."

"Yes, an' what are we goin' to look like by that
time?" said Mrs. Bott, determinedly pessimistic.
"Proper sights! I 'aven't 'ad no new clothes, not
for months. It's what I call a scandal, these 'ere
coopongs. I've lost 'eart even for 'ats. I'd like a
nice new 'at, but I 'aven't the 'eart to go choosin' one.
Droppin' to pieces, me clothes are, an' what does the
Government care? Nothin'!"

William put the last chocolate biscuit into his
mouth and, after a short frowning inspection of the
cake stand, whispered hoarsely to Violet Elizabeth:

"That jam roll looks jolly good."

Violet Elizabeth slipped from her seat and neatly
abstracted the jam roll from the cake stand.

Mrs. Bott was still bemoaning her fate.

"It's me birthday to-morrow," she was saying, "an'

d'you know what I'd choose for a present if I could
'ave it? I'd choose to come down to breakfast to
find a nice new 'at waitin' for me, an' to look out of
the window an' see flowers in the garden 'stead of
vegs, an' somethin' to get about on 'stead of me own
feet. I wouldn't mind 'ow short a time it lasted
if I could just see it once."

Violet Elizabeth seized William by the hand and
pulled him unceremoniously from the room.

"What did you do that for?" he said indistinctly
through a mouthful of jam roll as soon as they reached
the hall. "It's a jolly good jam roll and there were
four more pieces."

"I'll get you them afterwardth, William," said
Violet Elizabeth, and went on excitedly: "Did you
hear what thee thaid?"

"No," said William, "I wasn't listening. I was
thinkin' about the jam roll."

"Well, thee thaid that what thee wanted for a birthday prethent, wath to come down to breakfatht
to-morrow an' find a new hat an' flowerth in the
garden an' thomething to get about on 'thead of her
feet an' thee didn't care how thort a time it lathted. . . .
William, we could *do* that."

"I don't see how we could," said William. "We
can't get her a new hat, to start with."

"We *can*, William. Think of Mithith Monkth' hat."

William thought of Mrs. Monks' hat. Mrs. Monks
had bought a hat in Hadley the day before; it had had
to be altered, and, as Mrs. Brown was going into
Hadley later in the day, Mrs. Monks had asked her
to call for it and to send it round to the Vicarage the
next morning, as there might be no one at home that

evening.   So it had been arranged that William should
take it round first thing in the morning.

"You could eathily bring it here firtht, William,"
said Violet Elizabeth, "an' let her find it when thee
cometh down to breakfatht.   Thee thaid thee didn't
care how thort a time it lathted, tho you could
take it on to Mithith Monkth ath thoon ath thee'th
theen it."

William considered this doubtfully.

"What about the rest of it?" he said at last.   "What
about the flowers."

"Well, thee hath her breakfatht in the morning-
room an' all thee thees from the morning-room
window ith a little round bed with carroth and beetrooth
in.   We could pick thome flowerth from thomewhere
an' jutht thtick 'em in the ground with the carroth
and beetrooth.   You've got thome flowerth in your
garden, haven't you, William?"

"Y-yes.   Not many."

"Well, you can pick them an' bring them along
and thtick them in the ground and thee'll thee them
when thee cometh down for breakfatht."

"Yes, that's all very well," said William, "but what
about the other?   She said she wanted something to
ride on 'stead of her feet.   We can't get her *that*!"

"Yeth, we can," said Violet Elizabeth calmly.
"We can get her a nanny goat.   Thee thaid thee'd
alwayth wanted a nanny goat."

"But we haven't *got* a nanny goat," objected
William.

"No, but Farmer Jenkth hath.   He'th got Letty.
We'd only *borrow* her for a few minuth.   Juth for
her to thee when thee cometh down to breakfatht.

We'd tie her to that tree that thee can thee out of the window."

"He'd be mad if he found out," said William, "and she's a jolly funny-tempered goat, too."

"Thee hath good dayth, William. It might be one of her good dayth."

"Yes, an' it might not," said William.

"All right," said Violet Elizabeth with dignity. "If you don't want to help me, don't, an' I'll do it by mythelf."

William considered. Life was rather dull at present. His new friend, the sergeant, seemed to be confined to the camp and to constant attendance on Mr. Bloomin' Fuss-pot. It didn't look as if they'd ever get that walk in the woods that they had arranged. Time hung heavy on his hands, and, after all, any excitement was better than none. . . .

"All right," he said at last, "I'll help."

As he walked home he lingered by the camp, looking over the hedge in case his new friend was about. His new friend saw him, waved a greeting, and came over to the hedge.

"Like to know 'is latest?" he said. "Well, I've gotter spend to-morrow mornin' a-takin' photos of 'im with 'is camera for 'im to send 'ome. Crikey! You'd think with a mug like that 'e'd want to keep it dark. . . . 'Ere 'e comes. So long!"

Mrs. Bott came down to breakfast the next morning at her usual time. Her plump round face wore its usual morning expression of irascibility. At first she did not notice the gaily flowered hat box (discovered by William in Ethel's wardrobe) that stood on the

"WOT'S 'APPENED?" DEMANDED MRS. BOTT.

table just behind the teapot. When she saw it, she stared at it incredulously for a few moments, then drew off the lid . . . and stared still more incredulously at the new black straw hat that nestled there. As if of their own accord, her podgy little fingers drew out the hat and placed it on her head. She turned to the mirror that hung over the chimneypiece and began to try on the hat at various angles. Then an unaccustomed flash of colour caught her eye and she turned to the window. The small circular bed that had been patriotically devoted to the culture of carrots and beetroot, was gay with antirrhinums and sweet peas. Mrs. Bott's small eyes goggled. . . .

"Lawks!" she said. "Am I dreamin' or what?"

Then her eyes went beyond the bed to Letty, tied to the ornamental crab tree on the lawn, peacefully cropping the grass, and she sat down helplessly on the nearest chair.

"What's 'appened?" she demanded of the air round her. "Where am I?"

Receiving no reply, she opened the french window and, very slowly and cautiously, still wearing Mrs. Monks' hat, stepped out on to the lawn.

It had seemed to be one of Letty's good days when William and Violet Elizabeth "borrowed" her from the farm, but the sight of Mrs. Bott evidently exasperated her. She looked up from her cropping, and a wicked gleam came into her eyes. She was a strong goat, and the rope with which William and Violet Elizabeth had secured her was a weak one. Mrs. Bott had turned to go round the house in search of a gardener who might explain and deal with the situation, when the tornado struck her from behind. . . . A few moments later, Letty, wearing Mrs. Monks' hat rakishly over one ear, a spray of sweet peas protruding from one side of her mouth and of antirrhinums from the other, pranced gaily off into the shrubbery, leaving Mrs. Bott prostrate on the lawn, screaming for help. . . .

.   .   .   .   .

Captain Fortescue had taken half an hour posing himself for the first snapshot and was still not quite satisfied with the result.

"Stand just there with the camera," he barked to the sergeant, who was almost worn out by the nervous strain of the proceedings. "No, not there . . . *there* . . . and when I say 'three' pull the trigger down. . . . Stand a little more to the left . . . now a little to the right. . . . Wait a minute. . . . Come and take my place and I'll make sure it's all right. . . . Yes, that's all right. . . . Now change places. . . . No, it's not quite right. . . . Take a step forward. . . . Now

LETTY BUTTED THE CAPTAIN WITH JOYFUL ZEST.

you're too near. . . . Take a step backwards. . . .
Wait a minute . . . I think I'll have my other cap on. . . .
Fetch it from the tent. . . . Now we're all right. . . .
No, one minute . . . I'll have my field glasses in my
hand. . . . Fetch my field glasses. . . . Now we're
ready . . . No, you're not quite in the right position . . .
a little to the left . . . now a little forward. . . . No,
backwards and to the right. . . . One minute . . . I'll
have my gloves. . . . Fetch my gloves. . . . No, on
second thoughts, I won't have them. . . . Take them
back. . . . Hurry, hurry. . . . Don't take all day about
it, man. . . . Now are we ready? . . . Ready, steady.
. . . One, two, thr——"

The "three" ended in a high pitched squeal of terror.
Letty, pursued unavailingly by William and Violet
Elizabeth, had romped out of Mrs. Bott's garden
(leaving hat and flowers in the hedge) across two
fields, through another hedge, and into the field used
for the camp, where, attracted by the back view of
the gallant captain, she had butted into it with joyful
zest. Opinion was divided as to whether Sergeant
Malcolm had seen Letty coming and as to whether,
when Letty had made her presence both seen and felt,
he need still have taken the snapshot. The sergeant
himself said that he had not realised what was happening till it was too late, but, owing to the wink that
accompanied the statement, it did not carry conviction.
However that may be, the snap, as a snap, was a
complete success. It showed the captain prostrate
on the ground, his face distorted by terror, and Letty
standing proudly over him, her front paws on his
chest, his cap worn rakishly over one ear. . . .

.   .   .   .   .

William and Violet Elizabeth made their way from the scene of the crime as quietly and unobtrusively as possible, rescuing Mrs. Monks' hat on their way.

"Gosh!" said William. "That ole goat's jolly well messed everything up all right. What're we goin' to do now?"

"You thtay here," said Violet Elizabeth, "and I'll go and thee what'th happening at the camp. I don't think anyone thaw uth." She heaved a deep sigh of satisfaction. "It'th awfully exthiting, ithn't it, William?"

"It's all right for you," said William bitterly. "You've not got to take Mrs. Monks' hat to her, all messed up by that ole goat."

Violet Elizabeth crept off to reconnoitre and returned a few minutes later, smiling placidly.

"It'th all right, William," she said. "The captain'th rethting in hith tent and one of the tholdierth hath taken Letty back to the farm. Thee'th quite good again now. They don't know it wath uth. They think thee ethcaped."

"Yes, an' what about Mrs. Monks' hat?" said William sternly.

Violet Elizabeth's hunger for adventure seemed still unsatisfied.

"Oh yeth, William," she said eagerly. "Leth take it now and thee what thee thayth."

What Mrs. Monks said was unexpected and surprising. She took the hat from William's hands, inspected it closely, then tried it on in front of the hall mirror. She had bought a hat with a flat brim. The brim of this hat, thanks to its sojourn with Letty and its passage through a hedge, had taken on curves of the wildest nature. It dipped in the front and shot sharply up at the side. William watched apprehensively, but, instead of hardening into fury, Mrs. Monks' face softened into a coy smile.

"It's a much smarter shape than I'd realised," she said. "I think it suits me better than any other hat I've ever had. . . . Thank you for bringing it, dear boy, and here's a penny for your trouble."

But the most satisfactory result of the adventure was revealed the next evening, when William went down to watch the camp activities over the hedge. His sergeant friend came up to him. His harassed air was gone. He walked jauntily, and there was a twinkle in his eye.

"We had a bit of a mess-up here yesterday," he said. "P'raps you heard about it?"

"Y-yes, I heard about it," said William guardedly.

"Well, it's turned out a bit of all right for me," said his friend. "The photo's come out beautiful an' it's broke ole Fuss-pot's nerve. Broke it good an' proper. 'E don't know 'ow many of us 'ave copies, an' 'e can't think of nothin' else. Meek as milk, 'e's gone. Turn 'im round my little finger, I can now. We'll 'ave that walk in the woods any time you likes. . . ."

CHAPTER III

WILLIAM AND THE MOCK INVASION

GENERAL MOULT, wearing his Home Guard uniform, surveyed the small group of children whom he had summoned from the village and who were sitting on the floor and window-seat of his study.

General Moult had first seen service in the South African war, and his study was a South African museum in miniature. Native weapons, interspersed with mounted horns of various types of antelopes, covered the walls. A small chair was upholstered with a lion skin. An elephant's foot formed a waste-paper basket. A hoof of the general's favourite charger had been converted into an ink pot. A highly polished shell of ancient pattern did service as a letter weight. An enlarged photograph of a group of officers—showing the general, youthful, gallant-looking and generously moustached—was ingeniously framed in elephants' tusks. An enormous ostrich egg in a leather case with open doors stood on a book-case filled with books that dealt exclusively with the history, politics, flora and fauna of South Africa.

For the first two years of the present war the General, despite his Home Guard duties, had continued to regard it as an insignificant skirmish, but the forthcoming "mock invasion" seemed to have jerked him out of his rut. He had become so active and energetic and enthusiastic as to be almost an embarrassment to his fellow officers.

"We must leave nothing to chance," he said, twirling his white moustache belligerently. "I remember in the battle of Spion Kop . . ."

And now, on the eve of the "invasion," he had gathered together the junior inhabitants of the village—between the ages of ten and thirteen—and was giving them what he called their "orders for the day."

Their eyes roamed round the trophies, growing wider and wider, resting finally, at their widest, on the ostrich egg.

"You children," the General was saying, "are, of course, too young to join the Home Guard cadets, but that does not mean that you can do nothing to help in this invasion exercise. No child is too young to help his country. You must all try to do something to harass the enemy and assist the defending forces. Now I can't tell you what to do. Only circumstances can do that. But you must all try to take some active part in it, as far as you can. The enemy will be represented by regular soldiers, and the Home Guard, of course, will be the defenders. We'll have another meeting when it's all over, and I will ask each of you what you have done to help the defending force or hinder the enemy. I have decided to give the ostrich egg you see on the book-case as a prize to the child who has done most."

Again their gaze turned to the ostrich egg, and they stared at it, open mouthed, hardly able to believe that they had heard aright. The ostrich *egg*! The *ostrich* egg! It seemed impossible that one of them should actually possess the treasure.

"Bet I get it," muttered Hubert Lane.

They were unusually silent as they walked home. Each was living in a dream in which they captured paratroops, encircled whole divisions . . . won the ostrich egg. . . .

"Bet I get it," muttered Hubert Lane, again. "Bet you anythin' I get it. I'm jolly good at tricks."

"Bet you don't," said William. "I can do a few tricks myself."

"Huh!" snorted Hubert.

"Huh!" retorted William.

The next day, Sunday, was the day of the "mock invasion." Members of the Home Guard manned machine-guns in the ditches, and soldiers crept behind hedges with rifles in their hands. . . . William, filled with enthusiasm, tried to trip up a soldier and was soundly cuffed for his pains. He took part of his own dinner to a Home Guard manning a machine-gun near his home, only to have it thrown into the ditch with a "I know *that* trick. Read about it in the papers. You'll say I've been poisoned. . . ."

The day wore on and William became more and more depressed. No one seemed to want his help. He even tried to "immobilise" a soldier's bicycle by means of a pin but was caught, pin in hand, by the owner, from whose vengeance he narrowly escaped, as it seemed to him, with his life. He offered to help a Home Guard with his machine-gun but was told to go to blazes. To make things worse he met Hubert Lane, smiling smugly, at the corner of the road.

"Gen'ral Moult sent round to ask me for some maps of the district," said Hubert. "My father's got ten and I sent 'em all. I bet I get that egg."

**WILLIAM RAN INTO HUBERT LANE AT THE CORNER OF
THE ROAD.**

William walked gloomily homeward . . . but at his
gate he ran into a young man, who said breathlessly:

"General Moult's sent me to get any maps of the
district you have. Hurry up. He wants them at
once."

William brightened. Robert was an enthusiastic
motor-cyclist and had a large collection of maps . . .
He ran upstairs to Robert's bedroom and opened
the top drawer of his bureau. . . . Yes, there it was—
a long flat cardboard box with "Motoring Maps"

written on the outside. He had often seen Robert
taking maps from it or putting them back. William
had been forbidden to touch it, but even Robert
surely would want General Moult to have it in this
crisis. He put it under his arm and ran down
to the young man, who was still waiting by the
gate.

"Here they are!" he panted. "I don't know how
many there are."

"Thanks," said the young man and cycled off with
the box under his arm.

William went slowly in to tea. He wished he'd
opened the box and counted the maps. He'd like
to know whether he'd given more than Hubert Lane.
Anyway, he'd *given* them, and that was a weight off
his mind. Ole Hubert Lane had nothing on him now.
But, as he munched his way through the thick slices of
bread and margarine that formed his war-time tea,
a vague and ominous memory began to haunt his mind.
Had Robert, in those days of tension following Dunkirk
when a real invasion was hourly expected, said something about having hidden his maps? The vague
memory grew clearer. Robert *had* said something
about having hidden his maps. . . . Cramming the
last piece of bread and margarine hastily into his
mouth, he went upstairs to Robert's bedroom. If
Robert's maps were hidden, they must be hidden
somewhere in his bedroom. An exhaustive search—
whose effects nearly gave his mother a heart attack
when she entered the room the next morning—at
first revealed nothing, and William began to hope
that they were, after all, in the box that he had given
to General Moult's messenger. Then, idly and no

longer really expecting to find them, he took up the paper that covered the bottom of Robert's wardrobe.

There they were laid neatly out beneath it! His mouth dropped open in dismay. Gosh! He'd sent an empty box to General Moult and no maps at all. And Hubert Lane had sent ten. *Gosh!* He must find the young man at once and give him the maps. There was not a moment to be lost. Bundling them into his pocket, he ran downstairs and out into the road. There he looked anxiously up and down but saw no sign of the young man. He scoured the village and countryside, falling over stiles and scrambling through hedges in his haste, but still found no trace of the young man. His heart was now a leaden weight in the pit of his stomach. It wasn't so much the loss of the ostrich egg he minded, though he did mind that. It was the thought that he had failed his country in its hour of need, for William's vivid

imagination had by now transformed the "mock" invasion into a real one. His search for the young man brought him to the old barn. Passing it, he heard the sound of voices inside and peeped cautiously round the half-open door. General Moult and several other officers were sitting on packing-cases. It was evidently the headquarters of the Home Guard. At least, thought William, he could explain what had happened.

He entered the barn and approached the group of officers. "I say!" he began.

WILLIAM'S MOUTH DROPPED OPEN IN DISMAY.

General Moult looked up and glared ferociously. All the others looked up and glared ferociously. Someone said "*Get* out!" William, stumbling over a packing-case, got out. . . .

He went home, to find the maps no longer in his pocket. Somewhere in his scrambling over stiles and through hedges he must have lost them. Practically *given* them to the enemy—for it would be just his luck if a soldier and not a Home Guard found them. Gosh! Fate just seemed to have a down on him . . . Well, he couldn't leave things in the mess they were in. He must do *something* to retrieve the position. Then—quite suddenly—the idea came to him. Commandos. Why shouldn't there be Commandos in the invasion? Probably just because no one had thought of it. The Home Guard surely ought to have a few Commandos to help it. He'd be a Commando . . . It only needed a tin of blacking and a pair of bedroom slippers. He could easily get both. He proceeded to do so. It was the work of a few moments to abstract a tin of boot blacking from the kitchen, plaster his face with it, and put on his bedroom slippers. . . . Then he crept in conspiratorial fashion from the house. . . . It was unfortunate that he met Violet Elizabeth Bott at the gate. She gave a cry of delight when she saw him.

"Oh, William, you *do* look funny! What are you playing at?"

"I'm not playing at anythin'," said William sternly. "I'm a Commando in the invasion. Go away. I don't want you messing round."

"Can't I play, too, William?" pleaded Violet Elizabeth. "I like funny gameth."

"OH, WILLIAM, YOU *DO* LOOK FUNNY!" CRIED
VIOLET ELIZABETH.

"It's *not* a game," repeated William.

"Have you any more black thtuff?" said Violet
Elizabeth.

It turned out that William had. He had put the
tin into his pocket in case he had to renew his make-up
during the course of the evening. Reluctantly he
brought it out. Morosely he watched Violet Elizabeth
plaster her small face with it.

"Now I'm all black, too," she said happily. "What
thall 've play at?"

"I keep tellin' you, I'm not playin' at anythin'," said William impatiently. "I'm helpin' conquer the Germans."

"I'm thick of the Germanth," pouted Violet Elizabeth. "Leth pretend we're explorerth."

"I tell you I'm a commando," said William, "an' girls can't be them. They're too soppy."

"Girlth *aren't* thoppy, William," said Violet Elizabeth, stung by this insult to her sex. "I don't thee why they thouldn't be commandoth thame ath the Atth and Waacth and Wrenth. I'm going to be one, anyway, and you can't thtop me. I'm going to be a Waac. That meanth Women Auxiliary Commando. Girlth *aren't* thoppy, William. I'm going to be a Waac an' *help* you, thame ath the otherth do."

"It means goin' into danger—p'raps death," said William darkly.

"I don't mind," said Violet Elizabeth, dismissing death and danger with an airy gesture. "It'th a nithe game."

"I keep *tellin'* you it's not a game," snapped William. "I'm in earnest."

"All right," said Violet Elizabeth serenely, "I don't mind. I'll be in earnetht, too."

William sighed and yielded to the inevitable. He had tried to shake off Violet Elizabeth before and knew that it could not be done. After all, she would afford him a spectator for his exploits, and William liked to have a spectator for his exploits. . . .

He walked down the lane, Violet Elizabeth trotting beside him.

"Let'th play at being Robinthon Cruthoe and Friday," she suggested brightly.

William did not deign to answer.

"Well, let'th pretend we're ecthplorerth, then," she said. "It'th tho dull jutht being Commandoth."

"You wait," said William. "You wait till I get going."

"All right. What do we do firtht?"

"Well—er—I'll climb a tree and have a good look round for sentries then I'll creep up behind 'em and kill 'em."

"But I like thentrieth," objected Violet Elizabeth. "They're nithe."

"Well, I don't want you, anyway, an' I wish you'd go away . . . I'm goin' to go into this field an' climb this tree."

"Can I climb it, too?"

"No."

"All right. I don't mind. I alwayth get thtuck in treeth."

William went across the field to a large oak tree that grew by the farther hedge. He had often climbed it before and took only a few seconds to reach a good vantage point about half-way up. Violet Elizabeth waited patiently till he rejoined her.

"I got a jolly good view," he said excitedly. "I could see two men in khaki, guardin' things. One was guardin' the telephone box by the road an' the other was guardin' the bridge over the river. I could jump down on both of 'em an' overpower them, but I can't tell from here which is ours an' which is the enemy. I say! You go round an' find out which is which. See which of 'em's a reg'lar soldier an' which is a Home Guard. P'raps," hopefully, "they're both reg'lar soldiers an' I can overpower both of 'em.

Anyway, it's no good lettin' them see me before I start overpowerin' them or it'll put 'em on their guard. You go first an' find out which is which an' come back an' tell me an' then I'll go an' overpower whichever's the enemy."

"All right," agreed Violet Elizabeth and trotted off obediently.

William meantime searched for suitable weapons in the neighbouring hedge. He found a short stout stick with which, he thought, he could stun his opponent, and his pocket already contained a length of string with which he hoped to secure his victim when stunned.

Violet Elizabeth soon came trotting back.

"The one by the bridge ith a Home Guard, William," she said, "an' the one by the telephone bocth ith a reg'lar tholdier."

"All right," said William. "I'll overpower the one by the telephone box."

"Can I come, too?" asked Violet Elizabeth.

"No," said William firmly. "I'm goin' into deadly danger an' it's no place for women. Besides, you always mess things up."

"All right, William," said Violet Elizabeth with unexpected docility. "I'll wait for you here."

William crept across the field to the point in the road where the telephone box was. Carefully, silently, with the help of some railings at the side of the road, he climbed up to the top of the telephone box, then peeped cautiously over the top. All he could see was a netted tin hat, a khaki battle dress and an enormous pair of boots. The best way to overpower the enemy was, he had decided, to fling

WILLIAM LOOKED CAUTIOUSLY OVER THE TOP OF THE
TELEPHONE BOX.

himself down upon him from above and, while the enemy was still bewildered, stun and bind him. . . .

He waited breathlessly for a few seconds. Evidently the enemy, leaning against the telephone box in an attitude of extreme boredom, had not heard his approach. William set his teeth and drew a deep breath. . . . One, two, three. . . .

For a few seconds William and the khaki-clad figure rolled about the road in indistinguishable confusion. Unfortunately the figure in khaki recovered first from his confusion, dragged William to his feet and boxed his ears.

"You little devil, you!"

"Listen!" said William, rubbing his head, which had felt the full impact, first of the warrior's tin hat and then of his large and horny hand. "Listen! You don't understand. I'm a Commando an' I've captured you. At least, I dropped my stick when I fell off, but, if I'd got my stick, I'd've captured you, so——" he broke off, staring in amazement at the warrior's sleeve. "Gosh! You're a Home Guard!"

"'Course I'm a Home Guard," snapped the warrior. "And, let me tell you, you can get into serious trouble for interfering with a Home Guard in the pursuit of his duties. You may not know that this is an invasion practice, and that I'm guarding vital communications. I don't suppose you even know there's a war on. I suppose you think of nothing but your inane monkey tricks. Boys like you are a menace to the community. . . ."

"Listen," pleaded William again. "I was tryin' to help. I——"

But the Home Guard advanced upon him threateningly.

"Go home," he said. "Go home and wash your face."

William, in no condition to venture upon further hostilities, took ignominiously to flight.

He found Violet Elizabeth sitting under the tree where he had left her, sucking a piece of chocolate.

"Look here!" William accused her indignantly. "You made me attack the wrong side. He wasn't a reg'lar soldier."

"I know he wathn't," agreed Violet Elizabeth, mildly apologetic, "but I wath playing a *different* game—a game of my own. I wath pretending I wath an ecthplorer, theeing which were the friendly tribeth and the one by the bridge wath a *very* friendly one. He gave me a thlab of chocolate and I didn't want you to kill him, cauthe he wath tho nithe and kind, but the one by the telephone bocth wath very dithagreeable and wouldn't even thpeak to me, tho I wanted you to kill him, cauthe he wath tho croth. That'th why I told you he wath a reg'lar tholdier, cauthe I wanted you to kill him. He detherved to be killed for being tho nathty and croth."

William was beyond even remonstrance. He dug his hands into his pockets and trailed dejectedly homewards.

He was tempted not to attend the meeting at General Moult's house the next morning. He had nothing to offer but a record of failure and disgrace that would expose him to the triumphant jeering of his enemies for months to come. He hadn't even contributed a single map, and his encounter with the Home Guard was still a painful memory. It seemed, however, cowardly to shirk it, so, sore in both mind and body, he set out for the meeting.

Hubert Lane and his friends were already there, grinning complacently. They had all sent maps, and one of them, Hubert probably, would be sure to get the prize. William took his seat at the end of the row, his freckled face set and scowling. The ostrich egg still stood on the top of the book-case. It seemed to regard him with mingled derision and contempt.

"How many maps did you send the General, William?" said Hubert, and his friends sniggered in appreciation of the taunt.

General Moult entered and took his seat at his writing-desk.

"Now I'll ask you children, one by one, what you did yesterday to help the defending forces," he said. "I'll ask Hubert Lane first."

Hubert smirked triumphantly.

"I sent you ten maps," he said, "an' I bet no one else sent as many as that. My dad's always buying new maps. He buys jolly expensive ones, too."

General Moult passed on to the next without comment.

"I sent you three maps."

"I sent you four maps."

"I only sent one, but it was a jolly good one."

Hubert sat with his eyes fixed gloatingly on the ostrich egg. He would put it in the hall where everyone would see it as they came into the house, and he would tell everyone how he'd won it. If he wasn't in, his mother would tell them. No one had sent more

"AND WHAT ABOUT YOU, WILLIAM BROWN?"
ASKED THE GENERAL.

than ten maps.   He was sure of the prize.   He'd scored
over ole William Brown at last, and he wouldn't let
him forget it in a hurry.

"And what about you, William Brown?" the
General was saying.

William tried not to see Hubert's jeering face.   He
gulped and swallowed miserably.

"I tried to knock out one of the invaders," he said,
"but—but I got a Home Guard by mistake."

The General waved this aside.

"No real harm done," he said, "or I'd have heard
of it."   He cleared his throat and addressed his
audience.   "All you children, except one, have fallen
into a trap.   The man who came round asking for

c

maps and purporting to have come from me was a
fifth columnist. His aim was to procure maps for
the invaders and deplete the supply of maps available
for the defenders. Only one of you tumbled to the
fact that it might be a trick. That boy—realising, of
course, that to refuse outright would be dangerous—
very cunningly gave the man an empty box labelled
'Maps' then, just in case the message was a genuine
one, brought the maps round to me at Headquarters."
William gasped. The maps must have fallen out of
his pocket when he tumbled over the packing case in
the old barn. "I'm afraid I was rather abrupt on
that occasion, as I did not realise the object of the
boy's visit, but I congratulate you on your intelligence,
William Brown, and have much pleasure in presenting
you with the prize."

Dazedly William rose to his feet. Dazedly he
murmured thanks. Dazedly he took the precious case
under his arm. . . .

Violet Elizabeth accompanied him homeward,
smiling radiantly.

"I helped you win it, didn't I, William?" she said.
"It wath me that won it really, wathn't it, by helping
you overpower that dithagreable man that didn't
give me any chocolate."

And he was too dazed even to contradict her.

CHAPTER IV

WILLIAM'S WAR-TIME FUN FAIR

THE Outlaws fixed the notice on to the gate of the field, then stood back and examined it critically.

WAR-TIME HOLLYDAYS AT HOME FUN FAIR ENTRUNCE ONE HAPENNY.

"It looks jolly fine," said Ginger, who was chiefly responsible for its composition. (His English report last term had included the comment "Spelling atrocious.")

"Well, they ought to come to it all right," said William. "There's not much else for them to go to."

"Unless they go to Hubert Lane's," said Douglas.

"Yes, old copy cat!" said William. "Anyway, he can never think of anything to do."

"No, but he can get food for them, an' we can't."

"Well, I bet more'll come to ours than to his. It's somethin' to *do* they want now more'n food."

It had been William's idea to organise a "Holidays at Home Fun Fair" for the junior inhabitants of the village. The idea had been tried in the neighbouring town of Hadley on a large scale for the benefit of the adult population with great success, and William did not see why it should not be tried with equal success in his own village for the benefit of his contemporaries. Moreover, William fancied himself as a "showman," and in peace-time had organised many shows of one kind and another with various, and often unexpected results. Like many of his elders, he welcomed a chance of harnessing his own particular talent to the war effort.

The show was to be presented by the four Outlaws —William, Ginger, Henry and Douglas. Violet Elizabeth had had to be admitted to the organising committee for the simple reason that she refused to stay out of it. With the memory of the recent invasion practice fresh in his mind, William had at first firmly refused to allow her any share in the proceedings, but his firmness was not proof against her persistence.

"I'm not like that now," she had protested when William sternly reminded her of the "Mock Invasion." "I wath younger then, William. It'th nearly two weekth ago. I wouldn't meth thingth up like that now."

"All right," William conceded at last, "but you've gotter do what you're told."

"Of courth, William. I alwayth do," said Violet Elizabeth with disarming meekness and blatant untruthfulness.

As soon as the project was published in the village, Hubert Lane announced his intention of holding a rival show on the same day. William had expected this, of course, as the feud between the two boys and their respective followers was always ready to flare up at the least excuse, and the Hubert Laneites had not yet forgiven William for winning the ostrich egg.

"We needn't worry about *him*," said William again. "He can never think of anything to do."

"No, but he's got *food*," Ginger reminded him. For, though Hubert's brain certainly was not well stocked with ideas, his mother's store cupboard was, despite the war, well stocked with food, and the notice that Hubert put up to advertise his show contained the unusual and appealing word "Refreshments."

The Outlaws had decided to have their show in the old barn and the small field that surrounded it, and the Hubert Laneites were holding theirs on the piece of common ground that bordered the field.

"Gosh!" said Ginger, peeping through the hedge to watch Hubert's preparations. "He's put his garden tent up there, an' they've carryin' whole tins of buns and biscuits into it."

"Yes, but I bet he hasn't thought of anythin' to *do*," said William, "an' we jolly well won't let him into ours."

"Gosh, no!" agreed the others.

Mrs. Mason and her son Percival had moved recently into Honeysuckle Cottage. It was the first time that Mrs. Mason had been into the country for longer than a day, and she found the experience interesting. She was the sort of woman who finds any experience interesting, and not only finds it interesting but has to write an article about it. She was now engaged in writing an article on the Psychological Differences between the Town and Country Dweller. She went about the village all day trying to get "copy," but it was uphill work. People wouldn't, she complained, talk to her. . . . They refused even to describe the emotions roused in them by the sight of the common or garden cabbage or the domestic fowl. She had, however, taken copious notes on nothing in particular and was now engaged in working them up into an

article on nothing in particular. Therefore, when
Percival—long-legged and spectacled—asked for
permission to attend the "War-time Holidays at Home
Fun Fair" she gave it gladly.   Not only would it leave
her a clear afternoon for writing (Percival had an
enquiring mind and was fond of asking questions),
but it might also afford her some badly needed material
for her article.

"You'll tell me all about it when you come back,
won't you, dear?" she said.

"Yes, mother," said Percival.

Percival was a precise child and never embroidered
or added to a description.   His mother often said
that he had a "photographic mind."

Percival put his cap carefully and symmetrically
on his head (he was a very neat child, too) and set
off for the old barn.   A trickle of children was entering
the field, putting their halfpennies grudgingly and
suspiciously into an old cardboard boot box that
Douglas held out to them.

"Only hope it's goin' to be worth it," a red-haired
girl was saying darkly.   "I've been to lots of shows
of yours that weren't, let me tell you."

"Oh, those were in peace-time," said Douglas airily.
"This war-time one's jolly good.   Besides," he added,
hastily safeguarding himself and his colleagues
against possible contretemps, "you've not got to be
too particular in war-time. You've gotter show
patriotism in war-time by not bein' too particular.
It says so on the wireless."

"I've never heard it."

"Well, I think it says so," said Douglas uncertainly.
"It's always talkin' about 'sterity, anyway, an' this

is a very good show, but it's a 'sterity one, 'cause of the war.''

Percival paid his halfpenny and entered the field. A group of children was sitting on the grass, and William was addressing them through a megaphone improvised from a newspaper. Percival took his seat at the back of the group.

"Ladies an' gentlemen," shouted William, "the first item is a dog race between Jumble an' Hans. Jumble's my dog, an' Hans is Ginger's aunt's dog that we've borrowed for the race. He looks like a German dog, but he's not a Nazi one. He's same as a refugee. You know, the ones that come over in rowing boats. . . ."

"He *couldn't* row a boat," objected the girl with red hair. "He couldn't *possibly* row a boat. Not a dog. Well, have you ever *seen* a dog rowing a boat?"

"I never said he rowed a boat."

"You did."

"I didn't."

"You did."

"I didn't. I said he was *same* as the people that come over in rowing boats."

"How can he be the same? He's a *dog*."

"Oh, shut up! Anyway, the first item is this race between Jumble an' Hans. You can bet on it if you like, same as they do in the real ones. You can say 'Bet you a penny Jumble wins' or 'Bet you a penny Hans wins', an' so on, same as they do at the real races. . . . It's goin' to be a jolly excitin' race. They start when I blow the whistle an' you can cheer the one you've betted on, same as the real ones do. We've got a sort of war-time 'lectric hare for 'em that's

jolly good. It'll be the most excitin' race you've ever seen. . . ."

The red-haired girl snorted cynically, but there was a murmur of anticipation from the more credulous portion of the audience.

Percival sat and watched impassively.

"IT'LL BE THE MOST EXCITIN' RACE YOU'VE EVER
SEEN," SAID WILLIAM.

William held Jumble by the collar and Douglas
held Hans. Ginger brought a bicycle round from the
side of the old barn, to which Henry attached a dead
rat at the end of a piece of string. William blew his
whistle, the dogs were released and Ginger cycled
madly across the field, bumping from hummock to
hummock, the dead rat bumping along behind him.
Jumble, on being released, sat down and scratched

his ear. The dachshund trotted off in the opposite
direction to investigate the old barn. . . . One small
boy cheered but was promptly suppressed by his
neighbours. A murmur of disapprobation arose.

"Can't even race," said the red-haired girl, "an'
you said they could row boats."

"I never did," said William. "Anyway, they're
not used to racin' in war-time. We'll have it again.
They're jolly good dogs. They'll soon pick it up. . . ."

Ginger came back panting.

"What happened?" he said.

"They didn't get started prop'ly," explained William.
"They weren't quite ready. We'll give 'em a bit more
warnin' nex' time." He retrieved his megaphone,
now in process of being demolished by Jumble, and
applied the remains of it to his lips. "Ladies an'
gentlemen. . . ."

"Can't hear you with your mouth full of newspaper,"
said the red-haired girl.

"All right," said William, not wishing to enter into
further argument with such a redoubtable opponent
and realising that his megaphone was now more an
impediment than help to speech. "Ladies an' gentlemen," he crumpled up the remnants of his megaphone
and put it into his pocket, "Now listen. That race
was only a sort of rehearsal. We're goin' to have a
real one now. Get the 'lectric hare ready, Ginger.
Get hold of Hans, Douglas. Now let's give 'em a bit
more warnin' this time. One . . . two . . . three.
Go!"

Ginger bumped off again over the field. . . . William
gave Jumble a push. . . . Douglas gave Hans a push.
. . . Accepting these attentions as invitations to a

frolic, the two dogs leapt up exuberantly, mistaking a further succession of pushes for parts of the game.

Another and louder murmur of disapprobation rose from the audience.

Percival sat and watched impassively.

"*Cheatin*', that's what it is!" said the red-haired girl. "Gettin' us in here an' makin' us pay a whole ha'penny sayin' you've got performin' dogs rowin' boats an' all you've got is two balmy dogs doin' nothin' at all. I've got a *rabbit* at home that can act more sensible than those dogs, an' if you think——"

"All right, all right," William interrupted her pacifically. "It's not the sort of race you get in peace-time, I know. I'm not pretendin' it is. It's a war-time race, a '*sterity* race. You can't expect the same sort of race you get in peace-time. It's not— it's not patriotic to expect the same sort of race in war-time as you got in peace-time. I don't s'pose"— kindly—"you know much about war-time racin'. It's quite different from peace-time racin'. Same as oranges an' bananas, you know. Peace-time racin's one of the lux'ries we've gotter give up, same as Mr. Churchill told us." Even the red-haired girl was momentarily silenced by this, and William took advantage of her eclipse to continue hastily: "Now we'll get on to the nex' thing. The nex' thing is scenes out of hist'ry an' you've gotter guess what they are. There isn't a prize 'cause of war-time. They're jolly good ones, an' we've taken a lot of trouble over 'em. Now we'll have the first one."

He retired into the old barn, where the actors were making their preparations.

The first scene was to have been Raleigh putting his

coat over a puddle for Queen Elizabeth to walk on.
The only rehearsal had been a tempestuous one.   The
rôle of Queen Elizabeth fell naturally to Violet Elizabeth, and she had been difficult about it.   First she
had refused to walk on William's coat, saying that it
was a nasty dirty old coat and she'd rather walk in a
puddle.   Having decided that her own coat—a new

FORESTALLING WILLIAM, VIOLET ELIZABETH STEPPED
OVER THE PUDDLE.

one of mustard yellow—was more suitable to the occasion, she proceeded to blame the Outlaws because, owing to a long drought, there were no puddles for her to practice on. When Ginger made a puddle with water from the rain tub, she complained that it was too wet. The rehearsal had broken up with bitter recriminations on both sides, and there had been no time for another.

Things were in this unsatisfactory state when Violet Elizabeth emerged from the old barn, stepping haughtily and wearing a paper cap saved from a Christmas cracker. Simultaneously Ginger appeared round a corner of the barn, carrying a rusty old tin containing some muddy water scooped up from the ditch. William came round the other corner, the mustard yellow coat slung carelessly over his shoulder. Ginger emptied his canful of water at Violet Elizabeth's feet. Violet Elizabeth stopped and stared at the reddish slime.

"It'th all *muddy*," she said severely.

"Course it is," said Ginger. "It's gotter be."

"It'th not a real puddle at all," went on Violet Elizabeth, "an' it'th tho thmall I could *thtep* over it an' I'm goin' to."

Forestalling William, who was just taking the coat from his shoulders, she stepped over the "puddle," then beamed triumphantly at the audience.

"Now you've got to gueth what it wath," she said.

"You didn't do it *right*," objected William.

"Don't int'rupt," said Violet Elizabeth, and, to the audience: "Well, have you guethed?"

"Moses going over the Red Sea on dry foot," said Percival.

Violet Elizabeth considered this for a few moments then beamed delightedly.

"Yeth, it wath that," she said. "Yeth, that'th what it wath."

William shrugged helplessly.

"Well, you jolly well messed *that* up," he said. "Thank goodness you're not in the next one, anyway. Come on, Ginger."

They retired into the barn. Restive murmurs arose from the audience. The red-haired girl was heard to mutter something about getting her halfpenny back and going home if things didn't liven up pretty quick. . . . William emerged from the barn carrying three tennis balls in his hand. The scene was to be "Drake Playing Bowls while the Armada Sails up the Channel." Ginger, wearing a broad-brimmed felt hat belonging to his mother, was to represent the Armada in the person of its admiral.

William took up his position in view of the audience, put down two of the tennis balls and rubbed the remaining one between his hands as if transforming it to the necessary size and shape. Ginger, making rowing motions with his arms, came round the corner of the barn. William was stooping down to roll his "wood," when the threatening and too speedy approach of Ginger suddenly irritated him.

"You're comin' too close," he shouted. "Get *back*!" and flung the tennis ball at him, knocking off his hat.

"William Tell," said Percival.

There was a faint sound of clapping from the audience, mingled with a growing murmur of disapproval.

"*Fun* Fair!" said the girl with red hair bitterly.

"We've not had much *fun* so far. Come on, let's get
our money back and go home."

The audience rose to follow her lead. Douglas,
clasping his cardboard box, edged nervously away.
Too often in the past the Outlaws' shows had been
wrecked by a disappointed audience taking back its
entrance money by force and departing indignantly
home, after wreaking what physical revenge it could
on the persons of the organisers.

Percival, too far away to hear what was being said,
sat and watched impassively.

It was at this moment that the Hubert Laneites,
who had been interested spectators of the proceedings
through the hedge, chose to carry out their attack.
They outnumbered William's immediate followers, and
they judged rightly that the general feeling of his
audience was one of resentment, and that it would
form a ready-made band of allies. It was a glorious
chance of putting the Outlaws to flight and publicly
humiliating them.

"*Charge!*" shouted Hubert, dashing across the
field at the head of his band.

He was not prepared for his reception. Violet
Elizabeth, already worked up to a state of uncon-
trollable fury by her exclusion from the second
"historical scene" (she had hoped till the last moment
that she would be allowed to appear in it as the
Admiral's wife), welcomed this Heaven-sent outlet
for her rage. A tornado flung itself upon Hubert.
He found himself scratched, bitten and kicked by a
small flying creature who seemed to fasten upon every
part of his person at the same time. Howling with
rage, he turned to flee. His band, seeing their leader's

HUBERT LANE AND HIS BAND TURNED AND FLED.

flight, fled too. William and the Outlaws, recovering from their momentary amazement, pursued the Hubert Laneites with exultant shouts.

"Boadicea," said Percival.

The Outlaws' audience, welcoming this new excitement, plunged after them across the field and through the hedge. Percival followed slowly.

William had already invaded the tent, seized the tins of buns and biscuits and was handing them round.

"Thanks awfully, Hubert," he said genially. "They're jolly good."

Hubert cowered in the background, watching Violet Elizabeth apprehensively.

"Well, it's not a *bad* fun fair," conceded the girl with red hair patronisingly, taking half a monster doughnut at one masterly bite.

.   .   .   .   .

" And what was it like, dear? " said Percival's mother.

"It was quite enjoyable," said Percival. "First of all they had a war-time dog race where the dogs have to jump up instead of running. They did it very well. Then they had three historical scenes, and we had to guess what they represented. The first was Moses going over the Red Sea on dry foot, and the second was William Tell and the third was Boadicea. I guessed them all right. Then some children in the next field who were also having a war-time Holidays at Home Fun Fair came over to invite us to share their buns and biscuits, as we had none of our own. It was altogether quite enjoyable."

"Thank you, dear," said his mother. "That will come in very usefully for the article I'm writing."

She took up her pen and wrote: "Children in the country seem to have greater powers of co-operation than town children. They organise their own entertainments harmoniously without wrangling or dispute, and even rival organisations will unite in a friendly spirit to cope with war-time difficulties. At an entertainment my small son has just attended, organised entirely by the children of the village. . . ."

CHAPTER V

WILLIAM AND THE TEA-CAKE

IF it hadn't been for Mrs. Mason, no one in the village would have taken any notice of Fraulein Schmitt, or Miss Smith, as she preferred to be called. Miss Smith was an Austrian refugee, who had come to the Vicarage as a "help" about a year before the war— small, shy, timid and quiveringly anxious to justify her position. Moreover, her admiration of everything British was so extreme as to be almost embarrassing.

"Your calmness, your courage, your kindness," she would say, hands clasped, pale eyes brimming with tears, "they are an amazement to me. Constantly they are an amazement. Never in all my life have I been so happy as I am among you. After all my suffering it is like reaching haven after storm. My gratitude overwhelms me. Never do I wish to leave this beautiful country, these kind brave people. Here is my spiritual home."

The recipients of these compliments felt vaguely flattered but were, generally speaking, too busy to do anything about it beyond greeting her kindly when they met her scurrying about the village on her patriotic activities. These consisted chiefly of knitting innumerable sea boot stockings and helping at the local canteen that was patronised by large numbers of the airmen from Marleigh aerodrome. Mrs. Monks, her employer, gave her every afternoon "off," and Miss Smith spent them all at the canteen. It was difficult to get helpers for the afternoon shift, so Miss Smith took it on every day. She said that it was a small way of repaying all the kindness she had received in her beloved adopted country. . . . She never wanted to go anywhere else or do anything else and she had no friends. She kept the Vicarage in perfect order and cooked succulent meals out of nothing at all. Mrs. Monks called her a "treasure" and left it at that. It wasn't till Mrs. Mason came to the village that the limelight began to fall upon Miss Smith.

Mrs. Mason's journalistic genius had so far functioned chiefly in the atmosphere of Bloomsbury, but removal to the country seemed to have given it fresh impetus, and after a week or two, having exhausted every other topic connected with the village, she fell upon Miss Smith, the Grateful Refugee. Mrs. Mason pursued her indefatigably, interviewing her on her sufferings in her native land and on those feelings of gratitude to her adopted country that found such constant outlet in sea boot stockings and the local canteen. And then—when one would have thought that she had said all that could possibly be said on the subject—she discovered Miss Smith's soldier. Miss Smith's soldier was a tall stooping military-looking man, with a white moustache and a limp, who had moved from London at the beginning of the war and lived in rooms in Hadley. He took a "constitutional" into the country every afternoon, walking slowly and leaning heavily on his stick, and, passing the canteen, would often go in for a rest before continuing his walk. And Miss Smith adopted him. He became her soldier. He was a silent reserved man, but questioning would draw from him an account of how he had been gassed

and shot through the spine in the last war . . . and
to Miss Smith he typified all the other soldiers who
had suffered these things for her freedom.   Moreover,
he had been a prisoner of war in Germany and could
speak a little German, which he practiced with shy
pride upon Miss Smith.   Miss Smith discovered that
he had been born in Yorkshire and that one of his
happiest memories was the Yorkshire tea cakes that
his mother used to make. . . .   He had never tasted
anything to compare with them, he said, since he came
South. . . .   So, in order to give him a pleasant surprise,
Miss Smith set to work to make a Yorkshire tea-cake.
She hunted through recipe books; she experimented
on the Vicarage gas cooker . . . till she had at last
made a Yorkshire tea-cake that she considered fit to
be offered to him.   And he pronounced it good—as
good, in fact, as the tea-cakes his mother used to make.
Miss Smith's gratification was unbounded, and there-
after, whenever the soldier stopped at the canteen,
Miss Smith would have a tea-cake ready for him to
take home with him.   Mrs. Mason seized on the story
with zest and wrote an article—Fraulein Schmitt, the
Soldier and the Tea-Cakes—which appeared in one of
the monthly reviews.   After that, having exhausted
every other subject, she took refuge in those
happy hunting grounds of the journalist—War-time
Cookery and The Mistakes Our Generals Have Made
in Every Theatre of the War—and Miss Smith
relapsed into oblivion.

Not entirely into oblivion, however, for the story
of the tea-cake had somehow struck the popular
imagination.   Even Mrs. Brown, harassed as she was
by points and coupons, by the curious appearance of

war-time sausages and the still more curious disappearance of war-time eggs, found time to turn up an old cookery book and make a Yorkshire tea-cake.

"I think it's quite a success," she said modestly. "Anyway, will you take it down to the canteen for me, William? It's the day her soldier generally calls, I believe. I don't suppose it's as good as Miss Smith's, but tell Miss Smith that I'd like him to have it as well as hers, just to see if it's all right. If it is, I could make one or two occasionally to save her the trouble."

William had arranged to play in the woods with Ginger that afternoon, but, like everyone else in the village, he felt a proprietory pride in Miss Smith and her soldier, so he took the paper bag his mother gave him and set off for the Church Room, where the canteen was held. He found Miss Smith arranging cakes and teacups on long trestle tables.

"Mother sent you this for your soldier," said William, taking the tea-cake out of the bag and putting it on the table.

Miss Smith clasped her hands in ecstasy.

"But you are so kind," she said. "You are all so kind. I am so grateful, and my soldier, he will be so grateful, too. I will put it here, next to the one I have made myself, and he shall have them both. I am so glad to be here to give your kind mother's tea-cake to my friend. We have been doing what you call the Spring cleaning at the Vicarage, and I had almost decided not to come this afternnon, as we had reached the stairs, which, as you doubtless know, is in Spring cleaning a most difficult point, but dear Mrs. Monks insisted that I should have my usual time off this afternoon. 'Send for me,' I said, 'should any crisis occur and I will close the canteen and come.' She said she could manage perfectly, so I came."

William was on the point of taking his departure, when the small boy who represented the outdoor staff of the Vicarage appeared in the doorway.

"Please, Miss Smith, Mrs. Monks says she's very sorry to trouble you, after all, but could you come just a minute to give her a hand with the stair carpet? She's puttin' of it back an' got to the bend an' she says it's a bit tricky an' she says I'm not big enough to help an' she says could you close the canteen or get some-one to leave in charge just for a few minutes an' she's very sorry to trouble you."

The small boy paused for breath.

"Oh dear!" said Miss Smith, looking more put out than this simple message warranted. "Of course I will come at once. I do not like to close the canteen. It is true that few people come to the canteen at this so early hour, but I do not like that those who do should find a closed door." Her eye fell speculatively upon William. "I wonder . . . I will not be away long, dear boy, and few will come. Perhaps you would be kind to—what you say—hold the fort? No one will want more than a cup of tea and a cake. You can pour out a cup of tea from the teapot which I have freshly made, and the cakes are all on the plates set out. The cups of tea are a penny and the cakes are twopence. . . . And, of course, should my soldier come, this is the cake I have made for him." She took a paper bag from the shelf above the sink, opened it and showed a round tea-cake, floury and nicely browned. "You will give it to him, will you not,

"WILL YOU HOLD THE FORT, DEAR BOY?"
ASKED MISS SMITH.

my dear boy? Of course I may be back before he
comes. . . . I thank you, my dear boy, so kind and
good and helpful, like all the boys of your beloved
country."

With that she scurried away, leaving William to
"hold the fort." . . .

For a few minutes, William sat behind the teapot
waiting for customers. None came. He began to
grow bored. He began to grow hungry. To sit like

this, surrounded by plates of buns and cakes—jam
rolls, doughnuts, treacle tart, chocolate cake—was,
he thought pathetically, an ordeal such as few are
called upon to undergo in their country's service.
It was an ordeal, however, that he realised he must
undergo without flinching. The cakes belonged to
the Forces, and to rob the Forces of food was a crime
from which his soul shrank in horror. Like one of
the saints of old, he sat with his eyes resolutely turned
away from temptation—especially from the treacle
tart, which was his greatest weakness. But, as his
hunger grew, his thoughts began to turn to the tea-
cake that his mother had made. No question of
patriotism was involved in that. That question lay,
not between William and his country, but between
William and his mother. Miss Smith's soldier had,
of course, fought in the last war, but that was ancient
history now, and he had a shrewd idea that
Miss Smith's soldier did very well out of Miss Smith.
In any case, he would have Miss Smith's tea-cake,
which was all he was expecting. He took his mother's
tea-cake out of its bag and Miss Smith's tea-cake
out of its bag and laid them side by side on the shelf.
They looked very much alike. Perhaps one was a
little bigger than the other. If he were driven by the
pangs of hunger to eat one, he would eat the smaller
one, of course. . . .

The door opened, and he turned expectantly. A
customer or the old soldier? But it was neither. It
was Mrs. Mason. She entered, smiling coyly and carrying a paper bag in her hand. The smile faded from
her face when she saw William.

"I though Miss Smith would be here," she said.

"She's had to go to the Vicarage," explained William, "'cause of the stair carpet bendin', but she won't be long."

"Has her soldier been yet?" said Mrs. Mason.

"No, not yet," said William.

Mrs. Mason opened the paper bag and drew out a tea-cake.

"I've made a tea-cake for him," she said proudly. "I'm doing a column of war-time tea-cakes and I've tried them all, and I think this is the best. I'm so sorry Miss Smith isn't here. I'd stay and give it to him myself, but I'm going to Upper Marleigh to interview someone who has a new idea for Post-War Reconstruction—something to do with the Pyramids, I believe. It may, or may not, prove worth writing up. Anyway, here's the tea-cake. Tell him it's from the lady who wrote the article about him and give him my best wishes. And now I must fly. I hope that Miss Smith will be back soon, because I really—*really*—don't think that you are a suitable person to be left in charge of"—she waved her hand around her—"all this. However. . . ."

With that she vanished abruptly.

William took her tea-cake out of its bag and placed it with the others on the shelf. They were all so much alike that he could hardly tell which was which.

The door opened again. This time it was a customer —a despatch rider in crash helmet and leather jerkin who curtly demanded a cup of tea and piece of swiss roll. His heart swelling with pride, William poured out a cup of tea, put a piece of swiss roll on a plate, took the three pennies and dropped them into the till. The despatch rider was a man of few words. Displaying

no surprise at seeing a small boy in charge of the
canteen, he drank down his cup of tea in three gulps,
ate the swiss roll in two mouthfuls, said "Cheerio" and
vanished. The sight of the despatch rider's meal had
increased William's hunger. Its pangs had by now
become almost unbearable. He turned his eyes away
from the treacle tart and fixed them on the three tea-
cakes. By this time he hadn't any idea which was
which . . . but they looked jolly good. . . . After
all, one had been made by his mother, and he was
certain that, if she knew how hungry he was, she would
want him to have it. She could easily make another
for Miss Smith's soldier. In fact, the more he thought
about it, the more convinced he became that it was
his duty to eat it, if only to save himself from the
crime of eating the Forces' food. He didn't know,
of course, which of the three tea-cakes was his mother's,
and he didn't see that it mattered. They were all
tea-cakes, and surely one was enough for Miss Smith's
soldier. . . .

He took up the nearest and bit into it. Yes, it was
jolly good. He was munching away happily, when
suddenly his teeth struck something hard. . . . It
was a jolly big currant, or could it be a piece of candid
peel? He took it out of his mouth. Gosh! It was
an indiarubber—one of those long ones. *Gosh!* His
mother or whoever had made it must have dropped
it into the cake by mistake when she was making it.
Well, an indiarubber was a jolly useful thing to have,
and he didn't suppose she'd want it now. He'd
take it home and wash it. He slipped it into
his pocket and finished the tea-cake. . . . Yes, it
was *jolly* good! Fortified by it, he could even look

at the treacle tart without weakening. He put one of the remaining tea-cakes back into its bag and was just going to put away the other when the door opened again, and an old tramp sidled into the room. He was a picturesque tramp, with a tattered frock coat and a pair of trousers that still showed between rents and patches the remains of a black and white check and might even in days gone by have graced a Victorian wedding. In place of a collar he wore a dingy cotton handkerchief that might once have been red and his boots (he wore no socks) were tied together by string. What could be seen of his face through a covering of grime and several days' growth of beard wore a cheerful good-humoured expression.

"'Ullo," he greeted William. "Anythin' to eat?"

"It's only for soldiers," explained William.

"That's orl right," said the tramp easily, coming into the room and slinging a sort of bundle, tied up in old sacking, from his shoulder. "I fought in the Boer war *an'* the las' one, so if I'm not a soldier I don't know 'oo is." His eyes roved round the heaped plates. "Now wot've you got?"

"You've gotter pay for 'em," said William.

He tried to speak firmly but sounded weakly apologetic. He knew that tramps were considered undesirable characters and his own experience of them had not been encouraging, but they possessed an irresistible fascination for him. They represented that life of outlawry that had always appealed to him—a life of glorious freedom, unshackled by the trammels of respectability and civilisation. He would have liked to give this satisfying representative of the species the

"THIS 'ERE LOOKS A BIT OF ORL RIGHT,"
SAID THE TRAMP.

whole roomful of cakes, but he had to account for them to higher powers. . . .

"They're not mine," he added. "If they were mine I'd give them you, but they're for the Forces."

The tramp had drawn a battered leather purse from the recesses of his rags.

"Well, I can pay fer wot I eats, young 'un, same as anyone else. I've bin 'elpin' at a farm over Marleigh way, an' I got me wages."

"Well, a cup of tea's a penny and the cakes are twopence," said William.

He looked anxiously at the door as he spoke. He was aware that the presence of this customer in the canteen would not be approved by Authority, and he was eager to do what he could to satisfy him before Authority could intervene.

But the tramp was taking his time . . . wandering down the trestle-table, inspecting each plate in turn.

"The treacle tart looks jolly good," said William.

"Maybe," said the tramp. "I'll 'ave a good look round, anyways, an' see wot I fancies. . . ." His eye rested on the tea-cake that lay on the trestle-table in front of William's chair. "This 'ere looks a bit of orl right."

"You can't have that," said William. "That's for Miss Smith's soldier."

"An' 'oo may 'e be?" said the tramp indifferently. "Well, I jus' fancies that cake an' I don't fancy any of the others. 'Ow much is it?"

"It isn't for sale," said William.

The tramp shook his head.

"If a cake's displayed 'ere, it's fer sale," he said stubbornly. "That's the lor, young 'un. You can't refuse money fer somethin' wot's displayed fer sale same as this 'ere cake is, an' I've took a fancy to it. It's bigger than the others, an' I'm willin' to pay a bigger price fer it. 'Ow about fourpence?"

"B-but it's not for sale," said William again.

"Now, young 'un," said the tramp, "you can't refuse fourpence fer the funds of this 'ere canteen. Where's yer patriotism? This 'ere Mrs. Smith— 'ooever she is—won't grudge fourpence to a war heffort like this 'ere, nor will 'er soldier—'ooever 'e is. Not if they've got any patriotism. Mind you, four-pence is fourpence an' everyone wouldn't give it you fer a cake this size, but I've took a fancy to it. It's a *satisfyin'* lookin' sort of cake, the sort I used to 'ave when I was a child. . . . Well, make up yer mind quick, young 'un. If I wos you, I wouldn't like to take the responsibility of turning down a hoffer like this. I don't suppose 'ooever runs this 'ere show'll be pleased when they comes to 'ear of it. You don't get hoffered fourpence fer a cake hevery day."

William considered. After all, there would be one tea-cake left, and Miss Smith's soldier was not expect-ing more than one. To sell one to the tramp would be, as the tramp pointed out, fourpence clear profit to the canteen funds.

"All right," he said suddenly, "you can have it."

"Thanks, young 'un," said the tramp. "Now you can 'ave the satisfaction of thinkin' that you've give one of 'is Majesty's ole soldiers a treat *an'* made fourpence for the war heffort . . ." He opened the battered purse, put four pennies down on the trestle-table, slipped the cake into his bundle, then slung the bundle over his shoulder again. "Well, so long, young 'un."

He shuffled out, stopping at the doorway to light an old clay pipe. William went to the door and watched him wistfully as he took his way over the fields in the direction of Marleigh, his rags fluttering in the breeze. The attractions of every other imaginable career paled in comparison. After all, he considered,

THE OLD SOLDIER BEGAN TO TALK TO MISS SMITH
IN GERMAN.

brightening, once he was twenty-one, no one could stop him being a tramp if he wanted to. . . . Then he returned to the canteen and to the contemplation of his more immediate problems. Had he done right in selling the tea-cake to the tramp? Were the claims of Miss Smith's soldier more important than the claims of the canteen funds? Would he get into trouble if it were found out? Perhaps it never would be found out. Mrs. Mason was notoriously absent-minded. It probably depended on whether the Pyramid Post-War Reconstruction plan proved worthy of being written up. . . .

The door opened and Miss Smith's soldier entered, walking slowly and painfully, leaning on his stick.

"Miss Smith not here?" he said, looking round the canteen.

He had a quiet gentle voice that went well with his appearance of neatness and delicacy. There was about him the suggestion of one who had suffered illness and poverty but never lost his self-respect.

"She won't be long," said William. "She had to go back to the Vicarage 'cause of the bend in the stair carpet. She left the tea-cake for you."

The soldier smiled pleasantly at William.

"That's very kind of her," he said. "I'm sorry I can't wait to see her. I have to go back to Hadley. . . . You'll give her my thanks and grateful regards—won't you?—and tell her how sorry I was not to be able to stay and see her."

"Yes," said William, greatly impressed by the courtly bearing of the visitor.

He put the remaining cake into a bag and handed it over the table.

Still smiling pleasantly and drawing himself up for a ceremonious salute, Miss Smith's soldier took his departure.

William felt gratified at having participated in the little drama that had become so famous. His conscience still troubled him about the other two tea-cakes, but again he assured himself that the soldier had only expected one.

The minutes passed . . . Boredom and hunger once more began to claim him, but, before he could yield to either, Miss Smith came trotting into the room, her small face wearing its usual shy timid apologetic smile.

"I am so sorry to have left you for so long," she said. "It is kind of you to have stayed. The stair carpet proved difficult indeed at the bend, but dear kind Mrs. Monks and I have finally mastered it. . . . Has my soldier been?"

"Yes," said William. "I gave him your cake."

"That is good," said Miss Smith with what seemed to be a quick sigh of relief. "That is indeed good. I should not have liked the poor man to miss his tea-cake. . . . Well, my dear boy, I must not keep you longer." She took an apron from her bag and began to tie it round her waist. "I suppose you have not had many customers?"

"N-not many," said William and was wondering how to account for the extra fourpence without revealing that he had disposed of a tea-cake intended for the old soldier, when the door opened and the old soldier himself came in. He looked—different somehow. Less gentle and courteous. Less delicate. Even less old. He began to talk to Miss Smith in

D

German.   Miss Smith answered him in German.   Miss
Smith too seemed different.   Less timid, less meek
. . . but certainly not less anxious.   It must be talking
German that made them seem different, thought
William.

Then Miss Smith turned to him.   She was the old
Miss Smith, but, as it seemed, by an effort.

"You gave this gentleman the tea-cake I gave you
for him, did you not?" she said.

They watched him in silence, and in the silence
William was aware of a curious cold feeling travelling
up and down his spine.

"Not *exactly*," he admitted, deciding to make a

clean breast of it. "I ate the one my mother made an' Mrs. Mason brought another an' I sold it to an ole tramp for fourpence. You see, I thought——"

"Which way did he go?" cut in the soldier sharply,

MISS SMITH AND HER SOLDIER HAD ALMOST REACHED THE OLD BARN.

and again that curious cold shiver crept up and down William's spine.

"Up the field path towards Marleigh," said William.

"You little——" began the soldier fiercely, but Miss Smith shook her head at him warningly and turned to William with a graciousness and geniality that were somehow more terrifying than that momentary glimpse of anger had been.

"You have been so kind, dear boy, will you be even more kind and stay here while I and my friend just—er —return to the Vicarage to give Mrs. Monks a little further help? It will not take long with the two of us and we will be back soon. Good-bye for the present."

They had vanished before William could answer. He stood for a few moments considering the situation. He felt bewildered—so much bewildered that he could even look at the treacle tart with no other emotion than bewilderment. . . . He went to the door and looked down the road towards the Vicarage. It was empty. He looked up the fields towards Marleigh. Yes, there were Miss Smith and her soldier. . . . They were walking quickly. Miss Smith's soldier didn't seem lame any more. They had almost reached the old barn. He returned to the canteen more bewildered than ever and gazed unseeingly at the dainties around him. His bewilderment, he felt, was natural, What surprised him was that curious feeling of fear that still possessed him. How *could* he be afraid of sweet timid little Miss Smith and her gentle old soldier? But the fact remained that he had been and still was. Anyway, why were they going up the hill towards Marleigh, obviously following the tramp, when Miss Smith had plainly said that they were going to the Vicarage?

On an impulse William went out, closing the door behind him, and set off across the fields. There were no signs of the tramp, Miss Smith or Miss Smith's soldier. He was just passing the old barn when he thought he heard voices inside. He stopped. The door was shut, but there was a crack in it, and he approached cautiously, applying his eye to the crack. . . . At first he could hardly believe what he saw. The tramp was cowering in a corner of the barn and over him stood Miss Smith and her soldier. The soldier was only just recognisable. His face was set in lines that sent that shiver again up and down William's spine. And on Miss Smith's face, too, was a reflection of the cold savagery that had so transformed her soldier's.

"What have you done with it?" the soldier was saying.

"I dunno wot yer mean, guv'ner," whined the tramp. "I ain't done nuffin'. I ain't took nuffin'. You ain't got no right ter knock me abaht like this 'ere. I paid the little varmint fourpence fer me cake, I did. I can't 'elp it if 'e didn't oughter've sold it me. I've et it, I tell you. I can't give it you back."

"You know what I mean," said the soldier. "What have you done with it?"

"Give him something else to refresh his memory," said Miss Smith in that low vicious tone that was not Miss Smith's at all.

The soldier raised his fist and the tramp cowered down before him, whimpering, putting up his elbow to ward off the blow.

William turned and ran as fast as he could back to the village. By good luck a policeman was standing outside the general shop, idly examining a row of dusty birthday cards that had been there for the past eighteen months.

"Come quick!" gasped William. "Miss Smith's soldier's killin' the tramp."

The policeman turned and stared at him.

"*Killin'* him, I tell you," repeated William. "Come on quick or you'll be too late."

"None of your tricks, now," said the policeman, but there was something convincing about William's excitement, and, in any case, he was tired of the

MISS SMITH WAS CROUCHING IN AN ATTITUDE OF DISTRESS.

birthday cards. . . . He accompanied William across the field to the old barn.

"Go on! Look through the crack," urged William.

But this was, apparently, inconsistent with the dignity of the policeman. Instead, he put his shoulder to the large but insecure door and shoved it open. The scene it revealed was different from the one William had watched through the crack. The soldier was still standing over the tramp in a threatening attitude, but Miss Smith was now crouching on the ground in an attitude of distress. To William, it looked like a hastily-assumed attitude of distress, but he realised that to the policeman, seeing it for the first time, it must appear real enough. The soldier turned to the policemen. He was Miss Smith's soldier again—courteous, gentle, if a little stern.

"I'm glad you've come, officer," he said. "I found this brute assaulting Miss Smith. I heard her cries for help as I came up the field and I've been giving him a little of what he deserved."

"I ain't done nuffin', guv'ner," whined the tramp. He shuffled to his feet and came into the light, revealing a black eye and a bleeding nose. "I ain't done nuffin' an' look 'ow 'e's knocked me abaht. . . ."

"You brute!" sobbed Miss Smith.

The policemen laid an ungentle hand on the tramp's shoulder.

"You come along with me," he said sternly, and then, respectfully, to Miss Smith's soldier: "If you'll just give me the particulars, sir. . . ." He took out note-book and pencil. "You say you found this man assaulting Miss Smith?"

"Yes. Assaulting Miss Smith."

The policeman began to write slowly and laboriously.

"Ass-aulting . . . How many s's, sir?"

"Two."

"I gone and put three."

He began to hunt in his pocket. William suddenly remembered his newly acquired rubber and brought it out proudly, wiping the crumbs from it.

"Here's a rubber," he said.

The policeman took it, rubbed the offending s, then scowled suspiciously at William.

"None of your tricks!" he said. "This ain't no rubber. It don't rub, anyway."

"I thought it was," said William apologetically. "I found it in a tea-cake."

Then, for the first time, he noticed Miss Smith and her soldier. Their eyes were fixed in frozen horror on the rubber. Their faces had turned a greenish white. The policemen was still examining the rubber.

"Seems to have a sort of cap on," he said.

He took the cap off and pulled out a small roll of paper. Then the strangest event of the whole afternoon happened. For the tramp was no longer a tramp, except in appearance. He sprang at Miss Smith's soldier and pinned him in an expert grip from behind.

"Get the woman, constable," he said. "Don't let her go, whatever you do. . . . And you," to William, "cut down to the police station and tell them to send a car at once. My name's Finch. They know me. . . ."

The policeman was no less bewildered than William, but he recognised the voice of Authority when he heard it and sprang to Miss Smith, who fought and bit and scratched with unexpected ferocity before she was finally mastered. William, also recognising the voice of Authority, cut down to the police station. . . .

It turned out the Fräulein Schmitt did not, after all, love the "country of her adoption." She was, in fact, a fanatical Nazi agent who had come over among the refugees in order to carry on the work of espionage. Her soldier had not fought in the last war or in any other war. He was not even lame. He was the son of German parents who, though naturalised, had worked for the "Fatherland" ever since they came to England. It turned out that Miss Smith, hovering attentively over the airmen at the canteen while they ate their scrambled eggs or beans on toast, picked up a good many items of news that were of interest to the Fuehrer's representatives. These, together with other items that she picked up from the conversation of the officers who came to tea or dinner at the Vicarage, were carefully recorded in code, packed into a small asbestos container, in shape resembling a rubber, and baked into the "tea-cake" for which her "soldier" called each week.

Authority had for some time suspected Fräulein Schmitt of pro-enemy activity but could prove nothing. She wrote no letters and received no letters. She never left the neighbourhood and seemed to have no friends among the other refugees. It was Mrs. Mason's

THE TRAMP SPRANG AT MISS SMITH'S SOLDIER.

article that had first given Mr. Finch (of what is known as the Secret Service) the idea. There might be nothing in this tea-cake business, of course, but it was worth investigating. A stranger visiting the village would have caused comment and put Fräulein Schmitt on her guard. An old tramp, wandering through the village and cadging food at the canteen, would rouse no interest. He was lucky, of course, to find William there. . . .

"Why didn't you biff him one while he was knocking you about?" asked William when he heard the story. "I bet you could have done."

Mr. Finch grinned.

"I could have done, my boy, and, I can tell you, I wanted to, but I hadn't got hold of anything."

"You mean you hadn't got a clue?" said William, remembering his detective stories.

"I mean I hadn't got a clue," said Mr. Finch. "I felt that, if I held on, something might slip out that would give it to me."

"I gave it you," said William proudly.

"You did, my boy, and I'm grateful to you. . . . Good thing the bobby couldn't spell, eh?"

The news had already sped round the village. William walked homewards with a rollicking swagger. He would be famous now, he thought, for the rest of his life. . . . But he was too late. Already Mrs. Mason was typing her latest article: "How I Trapped a German Spy."

CHAPTER VI

ENTERTAINMENT PROVIDED

THE younger masters at William's school had vanished gradually with the course of the war, to be replaced by older men emerging often from the retirement of years. The new Maths master was half blind, and the new French master was more than half deaf, and the new Latin master so stiff with rheumatism that he could only walk with a stick. All three were such easy game that it was hardly worth trying to rag them.

The new history master, however, Mr. Polliter, was a very different proposition. He was old, like the rest, and, like the rest, he had retired from teaching many years before, but, unlike the rest, he was a distinguished scholar, who had the knack of making his subject interesting both to the expert and the lay mind. He was the author of several "best selling" biographies and a popular broadcaster on historical subjects. William, of course, did not know this. All he knew was that a subject that had consisted formerly of dates and maps and geneological tables and wholly uninteresting facts, had suddenly become alive and exciting—even more exciting than the Wild West stories with which he beguiled his leisure hours.

"Gosh!" he said when he came home from the school after the first lesson. "Did you know about this Napoleon chap? Gosh, it's jolly excitin'. Ole Polly was tellin' us about him ... There they were

sailin' out with four hundred an' eighty ships, an' none
of 'em knowin' where they were goin' 'cept ole Napoleon, an' all the time there was ole Nelson lookin' for
'em, an' then there came a storm, an' all the ships got
scattered, an' by the time he'd got 'em together again
ole Napoleon an' his fleet had nabbed Malta, an' then
ole Nelson went to look for him in Egypt, an' couldn't
find him 'cause he'd not got there yet, an' then there
was a sea battle an' ole Nelson won it, an' there was
ole Napoleon cut off in Egypt an' wonderin' what to
do next. . . . Corks! It seems an awful long time to
wait till next week to find out what happened."

Mrs. Brown looked at him helplessly. The situation
was without precedent.

"Are you sure you're feeling quite well, dear?"
she said.

"Course I am," said William. "Gosh! Jus' think
we've gotter wait till next week to find out what
happened when his fleet was sunk an' he was cut off
in Egypt."

"Surely you can read it in your history book, if you
really want to know," said Mrs. Brown.

"It's not the same in the hist'ry book," said William
simply.

Much to Mrs. Brown's surprise, this curious state of
things continued. Week after week, William came
home with fresh news of the Napoleonic wars—news
that was obviously more real and exciting to him than
the news that appeared in the daily papers.

He was describing to her one morning at lunch how
Napoleon had sailed in a small frigate without lights
right through the English fleet on his way back from
Egypt, when a letter from Ethel arrived.

"Ethel's coming home for forty-eight hours' leave," she announced when she had read it. "Just for one night. Oh dear! I'm afraid it will be very dull for her. There's simply *nobody* to ask in."

William thought of Ethel in pre-war days, moving always with a crowd of young men and maidens . . . from tea dance to dinner dance, from tennis court to swimming pool . . . on the river, in cars, on pillions . . . always with the same crowd of young people or with the chief boy friend of the moment in close attendance. Both girl friends and boy friends had now vanished from the village. . . .

"There's not a man in the place but the Vicar and General Moult," said Mrs. Brown." and they both bore her to death."

"I bet Mr. Polliter wouldn't bore her to death," said William. "I bet that if you could get him to come in an' tell her about Napoleon——"

"Don't be silly, William," said Mrs. Brown.

"But you've not *heard* him," persisted William. "I'd've thought it silly if I hadn't *heard* him. I bet if Ethel could hear him, she'd be *jolly* int'rested. I bet he's a lot more int'restin' than that ole Jimmie Moore an' Ronald Bell an' all the others she used to go about with."

Mrs. Brown, however, refused even to consider the suggestion, and William realised that her attitude was reasonable. No one who hadn't heard old Polly talking about Napoleon could have any idea how exciting it was. The best thing would be to get old Polly there by accident, as it were, and then everything would be all right and they'd all have a jolly evening. Poor Ethel worked very hard in the A.T.S., and

William felt that it was up to him to see that she had a good time the one evening she was at home. Nobody else seemed able to do anything about it.

"Oh, well," said Mrs. Brown finally," she'll just have to put up with it. After all, there's a war on. . . ."

All the more reason, thought William, why Ethel should be given a really enjoyable evening. The more he thought about it, in fact, the more determined he became to give her one. . . . And, contemplating the resources of the neighbourhood, he couldn't think of any more enjoyable evening than one spent in hearing from Mr. Polliter the thrilling exploits of the great Napoleon. Without much hope of success, he made another effort to enlist his mother's sympathy and co-operation.

"Mother," he said, "if you ask Mr. Polliter in for the evening Ethel's at home——"

"Now don't be silly, William," said Mrs. Brown. "Ethel doesn't want to meet any of those old school-masters, you may be sure of that. She doesn't like old men, and she doesn't like schoolmasters."

"But he's not an ord'rin'ry ole man, an' he's not an ordin'ry schoolmaster," said William, "an'——"

"Now that'll do, William," interrupted Mrs. Brown firmly. "Go and get the coals in."

As William performed his war time household chores, his determination to give Ethel an interesting evening through the instrumentality of Mr. Polliter increased. He realised that it was no use trying to make anyone understand who had not heard Mr. Polliter. The thing must be brought about by finesse, and William considered that he excelled in finesse.

At first it seemed easy enough. He would give

engagement calendar. "Tell your mother I'll come round after school on Tuesday and have a little talk with Ethel and see—well, see whether I think she'll be able to derive any benefit from the lessons."

Mr. Polliter saw no reason for disbelieving William's story. He knew William only as a small earnest boy who listened with almost devastating attention to every word of his lessons. Moreover, though vague and absent-minded, he had a personality that commanded respect, and neither college students nor school pupils ever ventured with him on that form of youthful persecution known as "ragging." It had suddenly occurred to William that even now Mr. Polliter might write to his mother. He gulped and swallowed again nervously.

"My mother said, would it be all right, her sendin' a message by me like this an' not writin'?"

"Yes, of course," said Mr. Polliter. "Tell her I quite understand, I never write an unnecessary letter myself on principle nowadays."

William walked home, feeling slightly dazed. Things so far had gone almost too smoothly, and he was only now beginning to realise how thorny was the path he still had to tread. He must prepare Ethel for her visitor, and that might very well prove the most difficult part of the whole undertaking.

Ethel, as Mrs. Brown had foreseen, was disappointed by the disappearance of all her friends from their old haunts.

"*Goodness!*" she said in a tone of deep disgust. "Isn't there *anyone* left here?"

"There really isn't, dear," said Mrs. Brown apologetically. "Oswald Franks and Hector Merridew and

Jameson are in the Middle East, and Jimmie Moor and Gordon Franklin and young Morency are in the Navy, and Ronald Bell's in Iceland. . . ."

"Oh, yes, I know," said Ethel carelessly. "I hear from most of them at intervals, but—*Goodness!* You'd think *someone* would have leave the same time as me."

William approached her after lunch when she was curled up in an armchair by the fire reading a detective story. He was glad to see that she was wearing her uniform.

"All my other clothes are so ghastly and out-of-date," she had said, "I simply wouldn't be seen in them."

Actually, though she would not have admitted it, Ethel had put on weight during her sojourn with the Forces and had tried without success to get into what she dashingly called her "civvies."

William approached her apprehensively, fully aware of the magnitude of the task before him. Ethel could not bear old men or schoolmasters, so he had to clear the expected guest of both these stigmas.

"There's an awfully int'restin' man at our school, Ethel," he began.

"U-hum," said Ethel absently without looking up.

"He's a *young* man," went on William," but he's gotter pretend he's old 'cause of secret work he's doin' for the gov'nment. He's gotter little beard—the kind they call Imperial—but he's dyed it white to pretend he's an old man an' he's got some chemical to take his hair off to make him look bald, but he's a *young* man really."

"U-hum," said Ethel again, turning over a page of her book.

"An' he's pretendin' to be a schoolmaster, but he's not really. He's gotter pretend to be one, 'cause of this secret work he's doin' for the gov'nment."

"What's he doing?" said Ethel, raising her eyes from her book.

William was nonplussed for a moment, then inspiration came.

"THERE'S AN AWFULLY INTERESTIN' MAN AT OUR SCHOOL," SAID WILLIAM.

"Well, the gov'nment heard that a lot of secret Nazi agents were gettin' posts as schoolmasters now that schoolmasters are so scarce an' doin' Nazi propaganda in schools to the children. Anyway, the gov'nment sent him down here to pretend to be an ole schoolmaster an' find out who was doin' it."

Ethel was listening now. After all, the story was not as incredible as the one she was reading.

"What's he called?" she asked.

"Polliter," said William, and, remembering Ethel's predilection for the higher ranks of the army, added: "Major Polliter. . . .   I say, Ethel," he went on after a moment's pause.

"Yes."

"I told him about you, an' he seemed jolly int'rested. I shouldn' be s'prised if he came round to see you."

Ethel tossed her red-gold curls.

"He wouldn't have the *impertinence!*" she said.

"Why not?" said William, surprised.

"I don't *know* the man."

"Well, you can't till he comes to see you, can you?" demanded William simply.

"No *gentleman*," said Ethel with hauteur," would just come to see a girl he's only heard of. If he couldn't get introduced in the ordinary way, he'd at least write and ask permission to call."

"Oh," said William rather blankly.

So he'd got to write a letter next. Gosh! If he'd known all the trouble it was going to be, giving Ethel a good time, he didn't think he'd have started on it. Still, he'd gone too far to retreat now. The situation, as situations usually did with William, had got out of hand. He must just write the letter. But he didn't

know what to say. He couldn't think what a young
man who has seen a young lady and wishes to call on
her would say. . . . Then suddenly he remembered
that on the top shelf of the bookcase in the study was
an ancient leather-bound book that had belonged to
his great-grandmother, called *Court Letter Writer.*
That might help him. Ethel was very particular
about good manners, and people had had good manners
in those days, all right. He'd seen them on the
pictures, bowing and being polite to each other all
over the place. He took the book up to his bedroom
and studied the index with frowning concentration.
"From a Young Lady to a Gentleman, Accusing him
of Infidelity" . . . That wouldn't do. . . . "From a
Diffident Lover to his Mistress." That wouldn't do. . . .
"From a Young Lady to a Gentleman Whom she
Could not Love but Whose Addresses her Parents had
Compelled her to Receive." That wouldn't do. . . .
Ah, *this* might do: "From a Gentleman of Inferior
Fortune to a Lady, Desiring the Honour of her ac-
quaintance." William turned up the page and,
translating the f's into s's with some difficulty, read:

"MADAM,

"Perhaps you will not be surprised to receive
a letter from a person who is unknown to you, when
you reflect how likely so charming a face may be to
create impertinence. Since I had the happiness,
madam, of sitting in the box adjoining yours at
the playhouse last night, I have been unhappy—
unhappy, because I had no prospect of attaining a
more intimate acquaintance with you unless it might
be by letter. No words can express what I feel, when

I tell you that, though a gentleman by birth, my
only dependence is an ensign's commission in the
army, and a legacy of about five hundred pounds left
me by an aunt.   I shall only add, dear madam, that
my happiness or misery depends upon the reception
with which this letter meets and that I am, with
unfeigned respect,

"Your most obedient,

"And most humble servant."

All he had to do was to change "sitting in the box
adjoining yours at the playhouse last night" to "seeing
you in Mr. Moss' sweet shop this afternoon" (for
Ethel had visited Mr. Moss to spend her sweet coupons), "ensign's" (whatever that was) to "Major's"
and sign the letter "Major Polliter."   He might as
well leave the aunt's legacy in.   For all he knew, Mr.
Polliter had one, and it might influence Ethel, who

was notoriously mercenary. Yes, it was a jolly good letter, thought William, reading it again appreciatively. He couldn't have made up a better one himself. He put Mr. Polliter's address and telephone number at the top of the notepaper and copied it out in small, fairly neat printed letters, giving much time and trouble to the process. Then he put it in an envelope and addressed it to "Miss Ethel Brown" in the same small printed letters. Even now, of course, finesse was needed. If he were to take the note in to Ethel himself, she would immediately connect him with it. He therefore placed it on the hall mat as if it had just

AN OLD MAN ETHEL HAD NEVER SEEN BEFORE
CAME INTO THE ROOM.

fallen from the letter box, feeling that a delicate and difficult task had been successfully accomplished.

It was an Ethel white with fury who rang up Mr. Polliter's telephone number a few moments later and demanded to speak to Major Polliter. Now it happened that Major Polliter, a young man of pleasant manners and prepossessing appearance, had just arrived to spend an unexpected leave in the god-forsaken little village where his father was carrying on his self-appointed war work of teaching. As his father was still in school, he answered the telephone.

"Is that Major Polliter?" asked an attractive but extremely haughty voice.

"Speaking," said Major Polliter.

"This is Miss Ethel Brown," said the voice. "I consider your letter a *gross* impertinence, and if you *dare* to come to the house I shall, of course, refuse to receive you."

"Hold on a minute——" began the Major, but Ethel, who was now thoroughly enjoying herself, interrupted. "And if you *dare* to speak to me in the village, I shall complain to the police."

With that she slammed down the receiver before the bewildered Major could gather breath to reply.

Mr. Polliter set out for his new coaching appointment immediately after school, and William took care to be hanging about the hall when he arrived.

"Good afternoon, sir," he said politely. "Ethel's in here. . . ." and ushered Mr. Polliter into the drawing room, where Ethel was curled up in an armchair in front of the fire, her detective novel on her knee. She wasn't really reading it. She didn't care two pins who'd murdered the man. She was so bored that she'd almost have welcomed a murderer herself. She was having a rotten leave. Her mother spent all her time in the kitchen, and there was nothing to do, and no one to talk to. She'd taken for granted that there would be one or two of the old gang within reach or home on leave. . . . And she felt not only bored but regretful. That voice on the telephone had sounded young and pleasant. She wished she'd asked him to come round for an explanation. William had said something rather exciting about his being engaged on secret government work. With everyone she knew away, he might have been better than nobody. . . . The letter had probably been meant as a joke, and if she'd only had the sense to take it the right way. . . . She had just come to this conclusion when the door opened, and an old man she had never seen before walked into the room.

Sitting there in the gloaming (it was after black-out time, and no one had bothered to draw the curtains and light up) in an armchair, her legs tucked up under her, her curly hair disordered, Ethel might well have been the age William had assigned her. The strange old man came across to her, put his hand on her curls and said kindly:

"So here's little Ethel in her A.T.S. uniform."

Ethel gave a strangled cry of terror and crouched back in her chair. Mr. Polliter was nonplussed. He had had no previous experience in dealing with mentally defective children and was afraid lest anything he might say should increase the little one's fear.

"Perhaps I'd better have a little talk with your

WILLIAM SHOWED THE MAJOR INTO THE
DRAWING ROOM.

parents first," he said uncertainly. "Where's your
mother, my dear?"

"In the kitchen," whispered Ethel, still overcome
by terror of this strange old man.

"Well, I daresay I can find her," said Mr. Polliter.
He went into the hall and, led by the unmistakable
smell of rabbit pie, made his way into the kitchen.

A few minutes later, William, hovering about the
hall apprehensively, opened the door again, this time
to a tall good-looking young soldier in major's uniform.

"Is Miss Ethel Brown at home?" he asked.

"Yes," said William. "She's in here."

The Major entered the drawing room.

"Miss Ethel Brown?" he said. "I'm Major Polliter. You rang me up this afternoon, and I felt sure that there must be some misunderstanding, so——"

Ethel saw William hovering in the doorway and went to close the door, followed by the appreciative gaze of Major Polliter.

William crept to the kitchen door and listened.

"But who on *earth* gave you the message?" he heard his mother say.

"William," said Mr. Polliter.

He crept to the door of the drawing room and listened. . . .

"But who on *earth* could have written it?" Ethel was saying.

The Major laughed.

"I don't know. All I know is that I'm very grateful to whoever did. . . . I say, are you *really* only at home for this one evening?"

"Yes, I'm afraid so. . . . Do tell me. Are you the Major Polliter who's here in disguise to investigate Nazi propaganda in schools?"

"Now look here," said the Major with another laugh. "Let's get to the bottom of all this. Who told you that?"

"William," said Ethel.

William reached out for his cap and tiptoed towards the front door. He realised that he had done what he had set out to do—assured Ethel an enjoyable time for her one evening's leave—but that no gratitude would be shown him, and that the best thing to do in the immediate circumstances was to go for a good long walk. . . .

CHAPTER VII

THE OUTLAWS' REPORT

WILLIAM plodded along the road, his school satchel over his shoulder, his hands in his pockets. He was collecting keys for metal salvage, and so far he had met with fairly good results. Large keys, little keys, rusty keys, bright keys, door keys, cupboard keys, attaché-case keys, jewel-case keys, ignition keys, jingled behind him as he walked. . . . But he wasn't thinking of keys. He was thinking of the conversations he had overheard at the houses where he had called. They had nearly all been on the same topic. . . . "Reconstruction" . . . "better conditions" . . . "shorter hours" . . . "higher wages" . . . "freedom from want and fear" . . . "the Beveridge Report" . . . His brow was deeply furrowed as he plodded along to the old barn, where he had arranged to meet the other Outlaws and compare results in key collecting.

Ginger, Douglas and Henry were already there when he arrived, engaged in counting their spoils.

"We've got over a hundred altogether so far," said Ginger excitedly. "How many have you got, William?"

William dumped his satchel down in a corner, still frowning abstractedly.

"Dunno," he said. "Look here! Everyone's talkin' about better conditions an' shorter hours an' things, an' what I want to know is what's goin' to happen to *us*?"

"What about?" said Henry.

"Well, everyone else is goin' to get a jolly good time after the war, but no one's thinkin' of *us*. Jus' 'cause we've not got a vote or anythin' we're not goin' to come in for any of it. What about shorter hours an' more money an' all the rest of it for *us*? I bet we could do with a bit of freedom from want an' fear, same as anyone else."

"Yes, I bet we could," agreed the others.

"I don't see why grown-ups should get everything an' us nothin'."

"How do grown-ups get it?" asked Douglas.

"They've got a thing called a Beveridge Report," explained William.

"Why can't we have one?"

"This Beveridge man's grown-up," said William bitterly. "So he only cares about grown-ups. We've gotter do somethin' for ourselves if we want anythin' done at all."

"The Outlaws' Report," suggested Henry.

"Yes, that's it. The Outlaws' Report. . . . An' we'd better get it goin' pretty quick. . . . Let's go to your house, Ginger. It's the nearest."

In Ginger's bedroom they squatted down on the floor to compose the terms of the Outlaws' Report, and Ginger tore the two middle pages from his Latin exercise-book and handed them to William.

"That'll do to write it down on," he said. "We've gotter have it same as theirs. . . ."

"Well, first of all, they're goin' to have shorter hours," said William. "So we'll have 'em too."

"Longer holidays," said Ginger.

"*Much* longer holidays," said Henry.

"As much holidays as term," said Douglas.

"*More* holidays than term," said Ginger.

"We'd better not ask for *too* much," said William, "or we may not get it. We'll ask for as much holidays as term. That's only fair. Well, it stands to reason that, when we've wore out our brains for—say, three months, we oughter have three months for our brains to grow back to their right size again. Well, you've only gotter think of trees an' things," vaguely. "They've got all winter to rest in. Their leaves come off at the end of summer an' don't come on again till the nex' summer, an' I bet our brains oughter be as important as a lot of ole leaves."

The Outlaws, deeply impressed by the logic of this argument, assented vociferously.

"Hollidays as long as term," wrote William slowly and laboriously.

"An' no afternoon school," suggested Ginger.

"Yes, no afternoon school," agreed William. "Afternoon school's not nat'ral. Well, come to that, school's not nat'ral at all. Look at animals. They don't go to school an' they get on all right. Still, I don't s'pose they'd let us give up school altogether, 'cause of schoolmasters havin' to have somethin' to do. Axshally, I don't see why schoolmasters shouldn't teach each other. It'd give 'em somethin' to do *an'* serve 'em right. Still, we'll be reas'nable. We'll jus' put down 'Holidays as long as term an' no afternoon school.' . . . Then there's 'Higher Wages.'"

"Yes," said Ginger, "that's jolly important. I could do with a bit of higher wages, all right."

"Let's say, 'Sixpence a week pocket money,'" suggested Henry.

"An' not to be took off for anythin'," said Ginger. "They're always takin' mine off me for nothin' at all. Jus' meanness. I bet they've made *pounds* out of me, takin' my pocket money off for nothin' at all."

"Yes, we'll put that in," said William, and wrote: "'Sixpence a week pocket munny, and not to be took off.' Now what comes next? What other Better Conditions do we want?"

"No Latin," said Ginger firmly.

"No French," said Douglas.

"No Arithmetic," said Henry.

"No, none of *them*," agreed William firmly, adding this fresh demand to the list. "I bet we can get on without *them*, all right."

"What about no hist'ry?" suggested Ginger.

"Well, we've gotter keep *somethin'* for schoolmasters to teach," said William indulgently. "Hist'ry isn't bad, an' English isn't bad, 'cause ole Sarky can't see what you're doin' at the back, an' Stinks isn't bad, 'cause you can get some jolly good bangs if you mix the wrong things together. We'll jus' keep it at, 'No Latin or French or Arithmetic.'"

"What else is there?" said Henry.

"Well, they're very particular about 'Freedom from Want an' Fear,'" said William. "We're gotter be particular about that, too."

"That means no punishments," said Douglas.

"Yes, that's only fair," said William. "*They* can break things an' be late for meals an' get cross and forget things an' answer each other back an' do what they like an' nothin' ever happens to *them*, so I don't

E

see why it should to us. It's about time *we* had a bit of this equality what people are always talkin' about."

"Well, let's put that down," said Ginger. "No punishments and stay up as late as we like."

"An' what about food?" said Douglas. "We'd better put down somethin' about that. We need somethin' more than sixpence a week to give us freedom from want. I bet I wouldn't feel free from want—not *really*, not *honestly* free from want—without six ice creams a day."

"*An'* bananas—after the war."

"*An'* cream buns."

"Yes, *an'* cream buns."

"An' bulls' eyes. Lots an' lots of them. As many as we want."

"An' we can't buy all that out of sixpence a week, so it ought to be extra."

"Yes, it jolly well oughter be extra."

They contemplated this blissful prospect in silence for some moments, then William said, "Now let's get it all put down prop'ly. Give us another piece of paper, Ginger."

Ginger tore several more sheets from the middle of his mutilated Latin exercise-book.

"It won't matter," he said carelessly, "'cause we won't be doin' Latin any more after we get this Report thing fixed up."

William took a sheet and wrote: "Outlaws' Report" at the head of it.

"They're goin' to make this Beveridge Report thing into an Act of Parliament," he said, "so we oughter do somethin' about gettin' ours made into one."

"What can we put that means that?" asked Ginger

They all looked at Henry, who was generally considered the best informed of the Outlaws.

"I think it's Habeas Corpus," said Henry. "That's somethin' to do with it anyway."

"No, it isn't. It's Magna Charta," said Douglas. "I'm *sure* it's Magna Charta."

"We'll put both in," said William pacifically, "so as to be on the safe side. How do you spell 'em?"

"Dunno," said Douglas, and Henry, who never liked to own himself at a loss, said airily: "Oh, jus' as they're pronounced."

Carefully, laboriously, William wrote:

Outlaws Report.
Habby. Ass. Corpuss.
Magner Carter.

1. As much hollidays as term.

2. No afternoon school.

3. Sixpence a week pocket munny and not to be took off.

4. No Latin no French no Arithmetick.

5. As much ice creem and banarnas and creem buns as we like free.

6. No punnishments and stay up as late as we like.

He looked up from his labours, frowning intently.

"Is there anythin' else?" he said.

The Outlaws drew deep breaths of ecstasy.

"No," said Ginger in a trance-like voice, "if we get that, it'll be all right. We'll be freed from want an' fear then, all right."

"Well, what do we do about it now?" said William.

They awoke slowly and reluctantly from dreams of unlimited ice cream, bananas and holidays. . . .

"We've gotter get it made into an Act of Parliament," said Ginger. "How do we start?"

"Well," said Henry rather uncertainly, "I suppose we've got to write to the Government about it."

"That wouldn't be any good," said William. "It never is. D'you remember when we wrote to the Government asking them to let us be commandos, an' they never even answered? An' the time we wrote to them, askin' them to shut all the schools an' send all the schoolmasters out to the war to finish it off quick, 'cause of them all bein' so savage, an' they never even answered that."

"We ought to take it to Parliament ourselves."

"They wouldn't let us in."

"Then we ought to give it to a Member of Parliament to take."

"That wouldn't be any good. There's only one Member of Parliament round here, and he's been mad at us ever since we tried to turn his collie into a French poodle."

"Then we've gotter find someone else high-up what's goin' to London to see the Government and will take it for us."

"I *know!*" said Ginger with a sudden shout. "There's Major Hamilton. He's high up in the War Office, an' he's been home for the week end, an' he's going back this mornin'. Let's ask him to take it."

The Outlaws' faces glowed with eagerness, then gradually the glow faded.

"That wouldn't be any good," said Douglas with a pessimism born of experience. "People don't take

"WE GOTTA GET IT MADE INTO AN ACT OF
PARLIAMENT," SAID WILLIAM.

any notice of children. It's jus' 'cause this ole Beveridge man's grown-up, that they make all this fuss of him. Ours is jus' as good, but I bet they won't take any notice of it."

"Let's go an' see, anyway," said William. "Where does he live?"

"Up at Marleigh," said Ginger. "He *might* be sens'ble enough to see that it's jus' as necess'ry for children to have improved conditions as what it is for grown-ups, but, of course," he ended gloomily, "he might not."

William folded up the document, slipped it into an envelope, wrote, "Outlaws Report. Pleese give to Parlyment" on the outside, and put it carefully into his pocket, then, accompanied by the other three Outlaws, made his way across the fields to Marleigh.

There, in front of a square Georgian house, stood a car laden with luggage.

"That's it," said Ginger excitedly. "That's where he lives an' he's goin' back to London to-day. His mother told mine he was."

A man with red tabs on the shoulders of his uniform hurried down to the car, threw a bag on to the top of the other bags and returned to the house.

He wore a lofty, supercilious expression, with a short moustache and an eyeglass.

"He looks high-up, all right," said William.

"But he doesn't look as if he'd take much notice of us," said Ginger, his excitement giving place to despondency.

"No, he doesn't," said William, inspecting him. "He doesn't look as if he'd even let us explain."

"He's got some jolly important papers with him,"

said Ginger. "He brought 'em home to go over, an'
he's takin' them back with him to-day. I heard his
mother tellin' mine that."

"*Gosh!*" said William excitedly. "*Tell* you what
we could do! We could jus' slip our Report in with
his papers an' it would go to the Government with
them an' be made an Act of Parliament. That's a
jolly good idea."

"But how're we goin' to slip it in with them?"

William surveyed the back of the car, piled up with
cases and rugs.

"I bet they're somewhere there," he said. "I bet
I could find them if I had a good look. I'll get in an'
have a try, anyway."

With that, William crept up to the car, opened the
door, and, crouching under a large rug that was hanging
down untidily from the back seat, began his investi-
gations among the cases that were piled there. Almost
immediately Major Hamilton came down the garden
path, leapt into the driving seat, waved his hand
carelessly towards the house and started the car. It
drove off, leaving the three remaining Outlaws staring
after it, their faces petrified by horror.

William was only slightly perturbed. The car
would be sure to stop somewhere for petrol or something, and then, having slipped his Report in among
Major Hamilton's other important papers, he would
make his way back as best he could. In fact, the
element of adventure in the situation was rather
exhilarating than otherwise. .... Very quietly—so as
not to attract the attention of the driver—he continued
to burrow among the cases. A locked attaché-case
seemed the most likely receptacle. Remembering the

satchel of keys that he still carried over his shoulder, he took it off and searched among it. Several keys seemed to be of suitable size. He tried them, one after another. The last one fitted. He opened the case. Yes, it was full of papers that looked important. He decided to put the Outlaws' Report at the bottom, so that it should be taken out with the others, and not

attract attention till it was presented to the Government along with them and, with luck, made automatically into an Act of Parliament. Turning the other papers out carelessly, he bundled them into his satchel, with a faint realisation of the fact that, though less important than the Report, they were still

THE CASE WAS FULL OF PAPERS THAT LOOKED IMPORTANT.

important, and must be kept carefully till they could be replaced in the attaché-case. He tried the Report in every position and at every angle, in order to find out which looked most impressive—right way up, with the words "Outlaws Report. Pleese Give to Parlyment" boldly displayed ... wrong way up ... sideways ... cornerways. ...

Suddenly the car began to slow down. Concerned for the safety of his precious manuscript, William hastily locked the attaché-case, then, concerned for his own safety, crouched beneath the rug. ...

The car stopped, and William, peeping from a corner of the rug, saw that it had drawn up in front of a hotel. Major Hamilton got out of the car and entered the hotel. William considered his next step. He had done what he had come to do, so he might as well return home before he was discovered. The Report was now on its way to the Government in London ... and presumably something would be done about it sooner or later.

Very cautiously, he slipped out of the car (on the side away from the hotel) and set off down the road. He'd probably find out where he was from a post office or something. He might even be able to "hitch hike" home, which would be a novel and enjoyable experience. A motor cyclist passed him, going at a breakneck speed. William put out his hand to stop him, but received only a scowl in reply. Oh well, probably something else would pass him soon, and he'd try again.

He walked on for a short distance then stopped, stunned by a sudden recollection. He'd still got Major Hamilton's papers in his satchel. Gosh! He'd better take them back again, or he'd be getting in a row with the Government, and it might even put them against the Outlaws' Report. He mustn't risk that. . . . Hastily he retraced his steps to the car. At the car he found Major Hamilton and a man who was evidently the manager of the hotel. Major Hamilton looked white and shaken.

"I was only in the hotel a minute or two," he was saying. "It was there on the seat of the car—a locked attaché-case—when I went in, and it's gone now. I must get in touch with the police at once."

"You didn't lock the car?" said the manager.

Major Hamilton grew paler than ever.

"I'd lost the key," he said. "I admit I took a chance. As I said, I wasn't in the hotel more than a minute or two and I thought I'd be able to see it from the window. I suppose that someone knew I'd got the papers and had been following me."

"What's been lost?" said William, pushing himself between them. "Your attaché-case?"

Major Hamilton looked at him, as if hoping against all reasonable hope that help might be forthcoming even from this unlikely source.

"Yes . . . Do you know anything about it? There were most important papers in it."

"I should think there were," said William indignantly. "There was our Report. Gosh! If *that's* been stolen . . ."

"What on earth are you talking about?" said the Major impatiently. "I'm speaking of important Government papers and . . ."

"Oh, them!" said William carelessly. "I've got *them* all right. I was jus' comin' to put 'em back."

With that, he slung off his satchel, took out the

papers and thrust them into the astonished Major's hand.

"I've got a lot of keys, too," he continued calmly. "I bet I could find one to fit your car."

There were long explanations, at the end of which (a key was actually found to fit the car) the Major took him into the hotel, gave him a meal that seemed to William one of pre-war magnificence and saw him into a 'bus that would take him home.

"No, I didn't get it to London," explained William to the Outlaws. "It was stole before we got there."

"Gosh!" said the Outlaws, impressed. "I shouldn't have thought anyone knew enough about it for that."

"Oh well," admitted William, "there were some other papers, too, but I bet it was our Report they were after really. Someone must have found out about it. . . ."

"Then we won't get an Act of Parliament?" said the Outlaws, disappointed.

"Well, p'raps not an Act of Parliament exactly," admitted William; "but this Major Hamilton says he'll do the best he can for us. He'll take us to a pantomime at Christmas."

The Outlaws' drooping spirits soared.

"A pantomime! *Gosh!*"

"*Hurrah!*"

For the Outlaws had acquired a certain philosophy of life and realised that a pantomime in the hand is worth a dozen Acts of Parliament in the bush. . . .

CHAPTER VIII

SOLDIERS FOR SALE

"IT'S goin' to be a funny sort of Christmas," said William. "No presents to buy, an' no money to buy 'em with."

"Some one told me to-day," said Ginger, "that you can get no end of money for old toys, now that they aren't makin' 'em any longer."

"Can you?" said William with interest. "Where do you take 'em?"

"Martin's, in Hadley. Victor Jameson got over ten shillin's for his train."

"Mine's all broke."

"So's mine. I took it this mornin' an' they wouldn't give me anythin' for it. But you can get a lot for toy soldiers."

William remembered the craze for toy soldiers that had swept the nurseries and schoolrooms of England at the beginning of the war. It had long since died down. In William's own bedroom was a drawer almost full of them, which was now never opened.

"Gosh!" said William. "I've got a lot of them. You have, too, haven't you? Let's put 'em all together an' take 'em down to Martin's."

Ginger frowned thoughtfully.

"I think we'd get more if we took 'em sep'rate. You start. You take yours to-morrow an' I'll take mine the day after."

"Right!" said William. "I want a bit of money to buy my mother a Christmas present."

"I heard of a boy what got a pound for his."

"Gosh!" said William. "I wouldn't mind a quarter of that."

"Well, anyway, you take yours to-morrow, an' I'll take mine the day after."

William pulled open the bottom drawer of his chest of drawers and emptied the medley of toy soldiers on to the floor. Though there were casualties among them, they were in not too bad a condition. A box full of Grenadier Guards was uninjured, the Colonel of a box of turbaned Indians had lost a leg and a sword, half a camel of an Arab regiment was missing, a private of Royal Marines was headless, a Major of the Buffs had lost most of his paint, several members of a crack cavalry corps rode on horses whose legs had been replaced by matches . . . but, on the whole, for the craze had been comparatively short-lived, the warriors were in good trim.

"Gosh!" said William, inspecting them. "Fancy if I got a pound for them!"

With a pound he could not only buy his mother a handsome Christmas present, but have a considerable sum in hand for various pressing needs of his own . . .

"Anyway," he added philosophically, "ten shillings would be jolly good. Or even five."

The next thing was to find a receptacle. He tried several paper bags, but their war-time quality was not proof against the weight of the soldiers. He went downstairs to the hall, where his mother's shopping-bag hung. It was a solid, capacious bag, made of a

gaily striped material, which had been brought from
Italy for her many years ago by a friend. It would
easily hold his army and conceal it from the gaze of
the curious.

"Mother!" he called.

"Yes," came Mrs. Brown's voice from the kitchen,
anxious and pre-occupied, for she was engaged on the
composition of a war-time cake of which she had had
her doubts from the beginning.

"Can I borrow your shopping-bag?"

"What for, dear?" said Mrs. Brown without much
interest. She was quite sure that there ought to be
more sugar in it. And less vanilla. She never did
trust these war-time recipes.

William hesitated. He had decided not to tell his
mother of the momentous commercial enterprise on
which he had embarked. It was better that the
handsome Christmas present, which its proceeds were
to provide for her, should come as a complete surprise.

"Jus' to go shoppin' with," he said carelessly.

"All right, dear," said Mrs. Brown, wondering if a
little nutmeg would improve the flavour. The War
Working Party was meeting at her house that afternoon
for tea, and she didn't want to be publicly disgraced.
Her cakes, after all, had been famous in peace time . . .

William walked into Hadley, spent some time gazing
at the puppies and rabbits in Emmett's window,
watched a practice "turn out" at the fire station, had
a passage of arms with a butcher's boy, then, summoning his resolution, made his way to Martin's. And
there he encountered his first set-back. The door
was closed and on it was printed a notice: "Closed
from 1 to 2 p.m. daily." William looked at the

church clock and found, to his surprise, that it was
ten minutes past one. The morning had slipped by
more quickly than he had realised. He was on the
point of turning away, when a boy of about sixteen,
with a pleasant friendly expression, came round the
side of the building.

"Hello," he said. "Do you want anything?"

William, ever ready to fraternise with and confide in
his fellow creatures, responded to this kindly interest.

"Well, he said, "I'd come to try'n' sell some toy
soldiers to Martin's, an' they've gone an' shut."

"Let's have a look at 'em," said the boy.

William handed him the striped shopping-bag, and
the boy held it open and inspected its contents.

"Someone told me about someone what'd got a
pound for theirs," said William.

"These are worth more than a pound," said the boy.

"Gosh!" said William.

"And—look here! It's an odd thing, but I'm
Mr. Martin's cousin, and I've come over to help him
with the shop for the Christmas rush. I've just been
fastening up the back of the shop, and I'm going to
have lunch with him now. Let me take the soldiers
and show them to him while we're having lunch. I'll
get more than a pound out of him, if possible. You
remind me of a kid brother of mine, and I'd like to do
all I can for you."

"Yes, but——" said William anxiously.

"There's nothing for you to worry about," said the
boy easily. "Leave it all to me. I can manage old
Martin, and I bet I'll get a jolly sight more than a
pound out of him. All you have to do is to come back
here at two and collect the money."

"Yes, but——" said William again, still more anxiously.

The boy, however, was already disappearing. He turned at the corner of the road to wave the bag reassuringly, then disappeared altogether.

"THESE ARE WORTH MORE THAN A POUND,"
SAID THE BOY.

William walked slowly and thoughtfully homeward. He supposed it was all right. It must be all right, of course ... Perhaps it would have been better to keep the soldiers ... but, on the other hand, he'd get more for them by letting Mr. Martin's cousin see to it for him. He *was* Mr. Martin's cousin, of course. He said he was Mr. Martin's cousin. He *must* be Mr. Martin's cousin ...

He remained thoughtful during lunch, but Mrs. Brown, too, was thoughtful and did not even remember to ask after her shopping-bag. Aunt Florence was coming to spend Christmas with them, and Mrs. Brown was a little worried about the rations. She was in treaty for a chicken and a rabbit, which would help out, of course, but Aunt Florence had a large appetite and lived at a hotel, and did not realise the mountainous difficulties that beset the housekeeper on every side. She was quite capable of eating up the whole family's ration of butter at breakfast the very first day and being quite unaware that she'd done so. Moreover, the War Working Party cake was definitely a failure. It was more of a pudding than a cake, and not much of a pudding ... So that she did not even ask William where he was going when he sloped out of the house immediately after lunch and set off at a brisk pace towards Hadley.

Entering Martin's, he looked round for Mr. Martin's cousin, but he was nowhere to be seen.

Mr. Martin came forward, smiling pleasantly.

"And what can I do for you to-day?"

"I've come about those toy soldiers," said William.

"Ah," said Mr. Martin. "Toy soldiers ... I'm afraid I have none in stock. The metal ones, of course, are no longer manufactured, and even wooden ones are difficult to procure."

William swallowed.

"I—I meant those I was trying to sell," he said.

"Ah," said Mr. Martin again, brightening. "Yes, I am always ready to buy them. Provided that they have not seen too much active service. Ha—ha! Yes, there is a good market for second hand toys at present. Have you brought them with you?"

"I gave them to your cousin this morning," said William.

"My cousin?" said Mr. Martin, his brightness fading into perplexity.

"Yes," said William desperately. "The shop was shut and he was outside it an' he said he was goin' to lunch with you, an' he'd take the soldiers for you to see, an' you'd give me the money this afternoon."

Mr. Martin looked at him in grave but kindly reproach.

"Now, little boy," he said, "I've no time for fairy tales this afternoon. You hardly expected me really to swallow a story like that, did you? To begin with, I haven't a cousin at all and——" He saw a customer enter and gently propelled William towards the door. "Now don't waste any more of my time, little boy. When you actually bring me some toys I shall be glad to make you an offer, but—— Yes, madam?"

William went out into the street, dazed and bewildered. His precious soldiers . . . his mother's Christmas present . . . not to speak of his mother's shopping-bag . . . He stood looking about him, wondering what to do next. He couldn't just tamely go home . . . No, he decided that he would have a good look round

Hadley first, and try and find the boy who had stolen his toys. His mother's shopping-bag was, at any rate, easily recognisable.

He walked round the back streets and the main streets and looked inside nearly all the shops, but found no traces of his mother's shopping-bag or the boy who had posed as Mr. Martin's cousin . . . And then just as he had given up hope and made his way to the bus stop in order to go home, his eyes fell upon the familiar striped shopping-bag, bulging with its contents. And it was carried by Mrs. Monks, the wife of the Vicar of William's own village, who was, like him, waiting for a bus.

He carefully avoided her notice, keeping to the back of the crowd and fixing his eyes on her intently. Mr. and Mrs. Monks led lives of such unblemished outward respectability—serving on committees, addressing meetings, supporting causes—that William, whose taste in literature tended to the lurid, had always cherished the suspicion that this blatant appearance of respectability hid some secret career of crime. He had—at different times and without success—tried to prove that they were spies, murderers and traffickers in drugs. And now, at last, his suspicions were proved correct. Mrs. Monks was a member of a Gang, if not the head of it. A Gang of Toy Stealers. Perhaps an international Gang of Toy Stealers. . . .

The boy who had posed as Mr. Martin's cousin was, of course, another member of the gang. He stole the toys, passed them on to her—in some crowded shop or fish queue perhaps—and she took them home and despatched them to the headquarters of the gang. Probably she was making thousands of pounds.

He remembered his mother saying only last week that she had appeared in church in another new hat, even more unbecoming than the last. Had it not been for his mother's shopping-bag, of course, he might never have discovered her secret. But he could not mistake the striped shopping-bag. He recognised even the grease spot on one side of it and the place where the handle had been mended.

He realised, of course, that it would be useless as well as dangerous to accuse Mrs. Monks openly of the theft. He knew that such gangs had means of getting rid of anyone who betrayed too great a knowledge of their activities. He remembered with a thrill of horror that an uncle of Mrs. Monks' had died quite recently, and that an old man in the village whom she used to visit regularly had died only last week. Probably both of them had discovered that she was the head of a gang. There was no doubt as to what he must do now. In dealing with criminals, one is justified in adopting their methods. He must somehow manage to steal the bag from her, as she had stolen it from him, and then, when that was done (he'd take it down to Martin's that afternoon), consider carefully his next step. Perhaps the best thing to do would be to write to Scotland Yard, though this would almost certainly expose him to the possibility of the criminal's revenge.

His spirits rising considerably at this prospect, he entered the bus behind Mrs. Monks, turning up his coat collar and pulling down his cap till they almost met, in order to escape detection, and sat down on the seat behind her. She put the striped shopping-bag on the empty seat by her side, then turned round

WILLIAM SNATCHED UP THE BAG.

to inspect the other passengers. Among them she saw Miss Milton, who sat on the same committees, supported the same causes, and, thought William sardonically, probably belonged to the same gang.

"Oh, there you are, my dear," said Mrs. Monks. "I wanted to ask you . . ."

Leaving the striped shopping-bag alone on the seat, she got up and went to sit next Miss Milton. Their heads nodded together. William, watching them as well as he could through the chink between his coat collar and cap, heard occasional isolated phrases: "Women's Institute . . . Choir practice . . . Canteen Committee . . ." Probably they were discussing the theft of the soldiers in code . . . Probably all these activities were so many blinds for the meetings of the gang.

The bus drew up at William's stopping-place, and a crowd of village women, who had spent the morning shopping in Hadley, passed down the gangway. William hesitated for a second, then, snatching up the bag from the seat in front of him, gently insinuated himself into the middle of the descending crowd of shoppers, and made his way unobtrusively homewards.

Upstairs in his bedroom, he poured out the contents of the bag upon the bed, but, to his amazement, instead of the avalanche of soldiers he expected, came a Christmas cake, some paper table napkins, ornamented by sprays of holly, a pan cleaner and a small china basket containing china flowers. He stood gazing at them in bewilderment. Then he looked at the bag. It was certainly his mother's shopping-bag. There were the grease marks and the mended handle . . . And it had been full of toy soldiers when last he saw it. It had presumably been full of toy soldiers when Mrs. Monks received it from the member of her gang. Of course, they did not stop at toys. They took everything they could. They'd been out shop-lifting or stealing all this morning, and this was Mrs. Monks' share. Naturally she wouldn't want toy soldiers. Not a bad share, thought William, regarding it critically . . . But it was jolly rotten for him. He'd lost both his toy soldiers and the chance of buying his mother a Christmas present. Then his brow cleared. The contents of the bag would provide an ideal Christmas present for his mother. That Mrs. Monks had presumably stolen them need not trouble anyone. His mother would not know . . . and, even if Mrs. Monks recognised them, she would not dare to claim them. He would start composing that letter to Scotland Yard to-night. . . .

William was never a boy to postpone any pleasureable sensation or dramatic scene. Christmas was not till next week, but, now that he'd got his mother's present, he might as well give it her at once and bask in her gratitude as long as possible. He packed the things back into the bag and took it downstairs.

"Here's your Christmas present, Mother," he said, handing her the bag. "I got it this morning."

Mrs. Brown unpacked the bag with exclamations of delight and surprise.

"Oh, William," she said, "they're *lovely!* How *sweet* of you!" William, wearing an expression of complacent magnanimity, allowed himself to be embraced, with further expressions of gratitude. "And now, dear," she went on, "you don't mind if I

"OH, WILLIAM!" CRIED MRS. BROWN, "HOW SWEET
OF YOU!"

use them all to-day instead of waiting for Christmas,
do you? It will make my little War Working Party
tea into a real Christmas party, and that cake I made
this morning is simply horrible. It tastes like cold
suet pudding. I don't believe that these people who
write war-time cookery recipes for the papers ever even
try them out ... We'll put the china ornament in
the middle of the table and use the table napkins and—
William, it's a lovely cake. Where *did* you manage
to get it?"

"Oh, I got it all right," said William carelessly.

"Well, we'll save some for you, of course. And a
pan cleaner! I've been trying to get one for months!

Well, now I expect you want to run off, dear. The War Working Party will be here any minute, and I know that you aren't any fonder of them than they are of you."

"Gosh, no!" said William, and vanished.

Mrs. Brown was so busy handing out wool that she had not much time to listen to the conversation of her working party. She was vaguely aware that Mrs. Monks was holding forth in a tone of virtuous indignation, but Mrs. Monks generally was holding forth in a tone of virtuous indignation. She had lost something, or had something stolen—Mrs. Brown wasn't sure which—and had called at the police station about it on her way to Mrs. Brown's. "Crime is on the increase," Mrs. Brown heard her say. "One finds it, I am horrified to learn, even in apparently respectable families. I shall certainly prosecute in this case, if the thief is found, no matter who he or she may turn out to be. . . ."

"Now will you all come in to tea?" said Mrs. Brown, putting away the wool. "It's war time, of course, but——"

"Oh, a Christmas cake!" said Miss Milton, as she entered the dining room. "How exciting!"

They all sat down, exclaiming appreciatively at the Christmas cake, the Christmas table napkins, the pretty china ornament. Only Mrs. Monks was silent, gazing from Christmas cake to table napkins, from table napkins to china ornament, with an expression that registered at first utter incredulity, then bewilderment, then the full fine flower of her righteous indignation.

"It's quite a pre-war cake," said Mrs. Parfitt delightedly. "Where *did* you get it?"

"Yes, where did you get it?" said Mrs. Monks in a voice that made them all turn and stare at her.

"It was a present," said Mrs. Brown, pleased by the sensation that her little tea-party was causing.

"And were the table napkins a present, too?" said Mrs. Monks in the same shrill trembling voice.

"Yes," said Mrs. Brown.

"*And* the china ornament?"

"Yes," said Mrs. Brown.

"Perhaps you've got a pan cleaner, too?" said Mrs. Monks.

"Yes, I have," said Mrs. Brown, surprised.

"*And* a striped linen shopping-bag?" said Mrs. Monks hysterically.

"Yes," said Mrs. Brown. "I've had that for years."

"For *years!*" echoed Mrs. Monks in a voice that died away in a squeak, then recovered itself. "*Indeed!* For *years!* May I see it, please?"

"Certainly," said Mrs. Brown, still more surprised. "I'll fetch it."

"For *years!*" said Mrs. Monks again with a wild laugh as Mrs. Brown left the room.

Miss Milton and Mrs. Claris exchanged glances. Only yesterday they had prophecied a nervous breakdown for Mrs. Monks, if she continued to overwork, "giving herself out incessantly," as Miss Milton put it, at the Women's Institute, the Mothers' Meetings, the Sunday School . . .

Mrs. Brown returned with the striped shopping-bag, which William had hung up again on its usual hook in the hall.

"This is my shopping-bag," she said.

"That is *my* shopping-bag," said Mrs. Monks, who had now got her tendency to hysterics in hand, and spoke in a deep, slow, resonant voice.

"Mrs. Monks, I've had it for years," said Mrs. Brown.

"Mrs. Brown, I bought it in Hadley this morning," said Mrs. Monks. "I bought it from a poor boy who was selling his mother's things to help pay for his sister's education. His mother had died last month. He told me the whole sad story in Hadley Market Square. I'd lost my own shopping-bag—I must have left it in some shop, I think—and he went round all the shops I'd been in, trying to find it for me, but unfortunately it had completely vanished. So he let me have this one. He even offered to *give* it to me because he said that I reminded him of his mother. He was such a polite boy. He apologised for the spot of grease and the torn handle. He said that the grease was candle grease because they were too poor to afford any other form of illumination, and the handle had got caught in the mangle once when he was doing his mother's washing for her . . ."

"The grease spot is lard," said Mrs. Brown indignantly. "The bag was on the kitchen table one morning when I was frying some potatoes. And the torn handle is where Jumble chewed it. . . . Really, I don't know what you're talking about, Mrs. Monks. Are you ill?"

"No, I am not ill," said Mrs. Monks, "though it's a wonder I'm not after all I've been through this afternoon. I'm not referring to the bag alone, Mrs. Brown. *That*"—pointing dramatically to the cake—"contains my rations of sugar and marge for *weeks* past. Not to

speak of the currants and candied peel and ground
almonds that I've had since before the war. I wanted
a really good Christmas cake, so I saved them up and
took them down to Miss Oldham of the Little Café
because she has a knack with cakes that I myself have
never been able to acquire. I called to fetch it this
morning. I couldn't possibly mistake it. *These*"—
pointing to the table napkins—"were for my own little
Christmas tea at home. *That*"—pointing to the china
ornament—"was intended as a Christmas present to a
dearly loved great-aunt. While the pan cleaner, the
pan cleaner——" Her self-control deserted her and
she broke into a sob. "I have searched for one all
this year. I have trailed from shop to shop, from
village to village for one, and at last to-day, after
simply *debasing* myself to the manager of Beltons'
Stores, I managed to secure one . . . only to have it
stolen from me under my very nose." She mastered
herself again and continued in a deep, strong, if slightly
unsteady voice: "Mrs. Brown, how long has this
pilfering been going on? These things were *stolen*
from me in the Hadley bus this morning. You say
they were a present to you. Who gave them to you?"

"William," said Mrs. Brown in a dazed voice. Then,
seeing William pass the window and hearing him open
the front door, called: "William!"

William entered and fixed a stern gaze on Mrs. Monks.

"William," said Mrs. Brown, "Mrs. Monks says that
all these things you gave me for Christmas were stolen
from her in the Hadley bus this morning. There must
be some mistake, because she even says my shopping-
bag was stolen from her, and you know how long I've
had that."

WILLIAM FIXED A STERN GAZE ON MRS. MONKS.

"Where did you get these things of mine?" said Mrs. Monks severely.

"Where did you get those things of *mine?*" said William with equal severity.

It was Mrs. Monks' turn to look dazed.

"What things?" she said.

"Those soldiers you stole off me in Hadley this mornin'," said William.

"*What?*" screamed Mrs. Monks, surrendering to hysterics again.

It was at this moment that Aunt Florence arrived. She was so pleased and excited that she failed to notice the strained expressions on the faces of those around her. She carried a shopping-bag of grey American cloth, heavily laden.

"My shopping-bag!" moaned Mrs. Monks, putting her hand to her head.

"Good afternoon, everybody," said Aunt Florence. "It's lovely to see you all again. William darling, I was so worried when I set out because I hadn't got a Christmas present for you. I simply couldn't find one anywhere. I stopped to look at a toy shop in Hadley, but there was simply nothing there. And then I met the most charming boy. He insisted on carrying my bag, though it was quite light, because really one takes little beyond a tooth brush anywhere these days. Anyway, this boy told me that he was trying to sell some old toy soldiers of his—in *quite* good condition—in aid of the Red Cross. *Such* a nice boy, he was. And it really seemed quite providential. Perhaps I paid him a little more than they're worth because the Red Cross is such a good Cause and he *gave* me the bag because he said I reminded him of his favourite aunt who'd died quite recently. . . . Anyway, here they are, William, and I *do* hope you'll like them. . . ."

She turned the bag upside-down on the sofa . . . and out they all tumbled—the Grenadier Guards, the legless turbaned colonel and his men, the half camel and his Arab rider, the Royal Marines with the headless private, the crack cavalry corps. . . .

CHAPTER IX

YOUTH ON THE PROW

WILLIAM had by now grown so much accustomed to the changes the war had brought to his immediate neighbourhood that sometimes he found it difficult to remember what it had been like before the war.

"Gosh!" he said to Ginger. "Won't it be funny without all these airmen an' Waafs about the place? It'll be—sort of dull in a way."

"An' there's goin' to be Ats too," said Ginger. "They're comin' to live in huts on the gun site on the common."

"Good!" said William. "It's time we had somethin' new."

"I b'lieve they're comin' to-night," said Ginger. "Let's go round an' see 'em."

Accompanied by Violet Elizabeth, they went down to the gun site that evening. They did not wish to be accompanied by Violet Elizabeth, and, in fact, did all they could to avoid her company, but Violet Elizabeth had decided to embrace the career of an At, and wished to cultivate the acquaintance of as many members as possible of that particular branch of the Services.

"It's silly, you thinkin' you're goin' to be an At," said William. "The war'll be over long before you're grown-up."

"It might not be," said Violet Elizabeth hopefully. "There wath a hundred yearth' war onth."

Most of the new-comers majestically ignored the three children pressing their noses inquisitively through the wire-netting that enclosed the gun site, but one of them came over and, with a friendly grin, popped an acid drop into each mouth through the wires.

"I'll be free to-morrow afternoon," she said. "S'pose you show me round the place. Woods and things." Her glance went up and down William's untidy tousled figure. "I've got a young brother at home like you—p'raps not quite so bad," she added with a twinkle.

Her name, she told them, was Patsy. She was the eldest of a family of seven and, as she put it, "couldn't help missing the little blighters." The other members of her "team" were sophisticated young women who found the countryside and its inhabitants equally uncongenial and whose one idea of pleasure was a "dinner and dance" at the Grand Hotel in Hadley with a suitable male escort. Patsy was so unlike them that it was with some surprise that William learnt she was engaged.

"What's he like?" he asked.

"He's nice," said Patsy. "And now come and show me the place where you have your wigwam."

She had a method of building a wigwam that far eclipsed the one they had always used. She could climb trees with astonishing agility and run as fast as William himself. She took them to the swimming baths in Hadley and taught them to play Water Leap Frog and Twisting. She was, for a grown-up, refreshingly human—untidy and haphazard, always losing things and forgetting things and being late for things. And she was uniformly cheerful and good-tempered and

F

generous. She shared her sweet ration with them.
She made bows and arrows for them—of a new and
improved fashion. She told them enthralling stories
about the adventures of her young band of brothers
at home. And—she warned them against Mrs. Sedley-
Mortimer. Mrs. Sedley-Mortimer was the originator of
the Youth on the Prow Movement and had written to
the Vicar suggesting that she should start a branch of
it in his parish. The Vicar, who disliked youth in any
form but felt a little guilty at not having himself done
anything about the Youth Movement idea that was
sweeping England, was glad that someone else should
shoulder the responsibility. He agreed with Mrs.
Sedley-Mortimer's main idea—that youth in war-time,
deprived in so many cases of parental control, needed
discipline and restraint.

"My Movement," she wrote, "is not for entertainment, but for inculcating the virtues of industry,
obedience and self-control. Too many of these Youth
Movements aim solely at filling in the young people's
time pleasantly. Mine has a higher function. It aims
at training the character."

With all of which the Vicar agreed so heartily that
he at once set about canvassing the local parents in
order to form the nucleus of his branch. The local
parents, harassed by war-time problems, were only too
willing to be relieved of their children's company
for two or three hours a week. Mrs. Brown enrolled
William as a member, and William, on first hearing of
it, was interested and gratified. He envisaged the
Youth on the Prow Movement as a sort of perpetual
party, with games and romps and buns for tea. It
was Patsy who disillusioned him.

"Mrs. Sedley-Mortimer?" she said with horror. "She's awful. She's a *menace*. She started one of her things in our village and the poor kids had a frightful time. She picks out the most terrible old frumps in the place to help her run it, and she visits every branch herself at least once a week, and—well, you wouldn't believe what it's like. They have to sit still and listen while she reads them lectures on the dullest subjects she can find. And you can't get out, once you're in. She's *ruthless*. She badgers the parents

"MRS. SEDLEY-MORTIMER IS A MENACE," SAID PATSY.

and even goes to fetch the wretched kids to the meetings herself if they don't turn up. . . ."

The news that the local branch of the Youth on the Prow Movement was to be run by Mrs. Monks and Miss Milton did nothing to cheer William and his friends. And they got little sympathy from their parents.

"Of *course* you must belong to it, William," said Mrs. Brown firmly. "I've definitely promised that you shall belong to it. . . . I don't care if it *is* dull. She's quite right. You need discipline. You're all running wild. I'm tired of getting complaints about you."

"It wasn't my fault about ole Miss Lomas's rabbits," pleaded William. "I didn't mean to let 'em out. I was only havin' a look at 'em. An' it wasn't really my fault about ole Miss Murgatroyd's aunt. I didn't mean to hit her ole aunt with that stone. I was only throwin' stones at that bit of her walnut tree that hangs over the road to get a few walnuts down. Well, you're *s'posed* to do all you can to get food in war-time, aren't you? I told her I was sorry one of the stones went over the wall into the garden an' hit her ole aunt an' I bet she needn't've made such a fuss about it. I've had bigger bangs than that without makin' a fuss. What would she do if the Germans came over, shootin' an' bayonetin', if she makes all that fuss about a stone?"

"Don't argue, William," said Mrs. Brown. "It's very kind of this Mrs. Sedley-Mortimer to take all this trouble, and the least we can do is to help her as much as we can. You must certainly join."

Ginger's mother was no more sympathetic than William's.

"She may teach you something useful," she said.

"She won't," said Ginger gloomily. "Not useful to me."

"Well, at any rate, we shall know where you are. If you're there you can't be careering over the country-side and annoying people."

"No, but I can be havin' a jolly rotten time."

"That's better than our getting letters of complaint from everyone we know."

"Well, I didn't mean to trample on Miss Milton's antimacassars——"

"Antirrhinums."

"Well, whatever they are. We were playin' at Highwaymen an' I was takin' a short cut through her garden to cut William off an' I jus' didn' see her anti-things. They hadn't any flowers on, anyway, an' I bet anyone would've took 'em for weeds. It's not fair to blame me for not knowin' every sort of flower in everyone's garden, especially when they've not got flowers on."

"Now, that'll do," said Ginger's mother firmly. "I shall insist on your going to all the meetings, so it's no good your making a fuss. It will do you good and give us a bit of peace."

Even Violet Elizabeth's mother, Mrs. Bott, a notoriously indulgent parent, insisted that Violet Elizabeth should join the Youth on the Prow Movement.

"I've got no time to look after you, love," she said. "And you can't get 'oliday governesses, not for love nor money, along of this war. A proper rough little girl you're gettin', goin' about with that there William Brown and his crew. I'm 'oping this 'ere Mrs. Sedley-Mortimer'll learn you to be a little lady."

Violet Elizabeth could generally be trusted to turn her mother round her finger, but on this occasion Mrs. Bott proved unexpectedly firm. As a wealthy and influential member of the community (for the community had long ago decided that what the Botts lacked in aitches was more than made up by their contributions to local Causes) she had received several gratifying letters from Mrs. Sedley-Mortimer, asking for her help and support in the Youth on the Prow Movement. Mrs. Sedley-Mortimer had hinted that Recognition from the Government might reward the supporters of the Movement, and Mrs. Bott had murmured "Dame Bott" dreamily to herself and wondered what an O.B.E. looked like. She even asked Mrs. Sedley-Mortimer to lunch on the day of the inaugural meeting, although it meant opening her last remaining tin of Luncheon Meat. . . .

From Patsy at least the Outlaws and Violet Elizabeth hoped for sympathy, but Patsy had troubles of her own and less interest than usual to spare for theirs. Patsy's fiancé had been given a few days' leave and was coming to spend it at the village pub, so as to be near Patsy. And Patsy had run out of cosmetics. . . .

"We're allowed to spend three-and-six a month on the stuff," she said, "and I got mine right at the beginning of the month and I've finished it all and I've had two of the kids' birthdays this last week and haven't a cent left. And he hasn't seen me for ages, so I don't want to give him too much of a shock. He'll be wondering what came over him to ask me to marry him. I know I look frightful without it. Gosh! I wish I could get hold of some."

William and Ginger tried conscientiously to sympathise with her, but it was, naturally, Violet Elizabeth who constituted herself the champion of her sex.

"We'll get thome for you," she said, her lisp accentuated by her earnestness. "Tell you what! I'll get thome of my mother'th for you."

"You can't," said Patsy gloomily. "The stuff's so precious these days that she'd know if a *grain* went."

Violet Elizabeth considered the question frowningly, then her brow cleared.

"I *know*!" she said. "Thee's got thome in a drething-cathe that thee only utheth when thee goeth away. Thee'th not been away for tho long that I ethpect thee's forgotten thee's got it. I'll bring it and we'll have a look at it."

"All right," said Patsy, "but," apprehensively, "don't let her see or know you've got it."

"Oh, no," said Violet Elizabeth. "Thee'th got that thilly woman coming to lunth and thee can't think of anything elth. I bet there'th loth and *loth* of the thtuff in that cathe."

"It's very kind of you," said Patsy. "I know it all seems soppy to you," she went on apologetically to William and Ginger, "but—but it *does* matter to me."

"Y-yes, I bet it does," said William indulgently, and added, with an air of worldly wisdom: "I've seen it on the pictures an' I bet you can't help it. I know you aren't *really* soppy."

"You bring boctheth for them," said Violet Elizabeth to Patsy, "then we can take them out of *her* boctheth and put them into yourth, tho that if thee lookth at her cathe thee'll thee the boctheth thtill there and think it'th all right."

"It's awfully good of you and I do hope you don't

"HERE IT ITH," SAID VIOLET ELIZABETH.

mind," said Patsy. "I feel it's dreadful of me to
bother you with this just when you're in such trouble
yourselves."

"It'll give us something else to think of," said
William, "before she starts on us."

"We'll meet at the end of the thrubbery to-morrow
morning at twelve o'clock," said Violet Elizabeth, who
was enjoying the conspiratorial element in the situation
and was inclined to overdo it. "I'll bring the cathe
and you bring your boctheth. We'd better have a

pathword. Do you think we ought to wear mathkth? We don't want to be dithcovered."

"I don't think that masks are really necessary," said Patsy, "but we'll all come by different ways, shall we?"

"Yeth," said Violet Elizabeth happily, "tho ath not to arouthe thuthpithion."

They met in the shrubbery the next morning—Violet Elizabeth slipping from tree to tree, taking cover every moment from imaginary spies, holding the small pig-skin, zip-fastened case beneath her cardigan. Patsy carried an attaché-case, and William and Ginger attended moodily, the thought of the afternoon's meeting hanging over their spirits like a black cloud.

"Here it ith," said Violet Elizabeth, squatting on the ground, putting the case in front of her and opening the zip-fastener. Patsy sat down beside her, watching expectantly.

"Has that awful woman come yet?" groaned William.

"Not yet," said Violet Elizabeth, "but theeth coming for lunth and thee and my mother are going to the Vicarage to tea after the meeting. The Bithop'th going to be at the Vicarage and my mother'th ecthited 'cauthe thee liketh high-up people and thee thinkth bithopth are high-up."

Patsy, who had opened the case, gave a gasp of delight.

"They're *lovely*," she said. "But they're all new. They haven't even been opened. Oh, I'm sure I oughtn't to take any."

"Yeth, you take 'em," said Violet Elizabeth generously. "You take 'em all. I don't want 'em."

"But what about your mother?"

"Thee won't know. Not for ageth. Thee only uthes that cathe when thee goeth away and thee'th not going away again thith year."

"I'll save up and pay them back," said Patsy. "I'll have them all put back by the time she needs them."

"No, don't you bother," said Violet Elizabeth, still with her air of careless munificence.

"But I *will*," said Patsy earnestly. "I'll pay it all back. It would be stealing if I didn't. And if she finds out before that, you'll tell me, won't you? I don't want anyone else to get into trouble for it."

"Thee won't find out," said Violet Elizabeth serenely. "I've got an idea about that. Take 'em all."

"No, I only want the vanishing cream and powder and rouge and lipstick. I don't want any of those lotions and things."

"All right. . . ."

Violet Elizabeth carefully transferred the contents of the jar of vanishing cream, the box of powder, the rouge and lipstick into Patsy's receptacles and closed the case. "And you needn't pay them back cauthe of thith idea I've got."

"Well," said Patsy, fastening up her attaché-case briskly, "I'm awfully grateful to you and I'm sorry I've wasted so much of your morning. There's just time to go to the woods before lunch."

"And before that awful woman comes," said William, rising with alacrity.

"I won't come with you," said Violet Elizabeth mysteriously. "I've got thingth to do. It'th about thith idea. . . ."

Wholly uninterested in Violet Elizabeth's idea, they ran off to the woods. . . .

For some minutes Violet Elizabeth stayed where she was, sitting in the shade of a variegated laurel and gazing thoughtfully at the pigskin case. The idea had come to her suddenly while she was carrying her mother's dressing-case down to the shrubbery and needed a little further consideration. She did not want Patsy to have to pay back any of the "borrowed" cosmetics, but she foresaw trouble, should her mother chance to look into the case and find so many of its contents missing. The "idea" was to replace them in such a way that her mother, opening them for the first time, should imagine that the manufacturers had made some mistake and sent the wrong articles. Then only the manufacturers (with whom Violet Elizabeth was not concerned) would get into trouble and Patsy need not replace anything.

She carried the case up to her bedroom, took out the empty jars and considered them, still frowning thoughtfully. She'd fill the vanishing cream jar first. Lard would do. . . . Or perhaps butter. . . . She went cautiously downstairs to the kitchen. No, it wasn't any use. The kitchen was in the throes of preparation for Mrs. Sedley-Mortimer's lunch. It would be impossible even to approach the larder without being seen and questioned. She was passing the side door on her way back to the staircase when she saw, on the floor of the side porch, a tin of red paste used by the charwoman for polishing the red tiles. That, surely, thought Violet Elizabeth, would do as well as anything else. She had a vague idea that the original contents had been white, but, after all, most of these face things were pink, and it didn't make much difference. Hastily she filled the jar with it, took it upstairs and replaced it in the case. The next was the powder box. That was easier. Powder was very like dust. In fact, Mrs. Bott might even think that it had once been powder but had deteriorated through disuse. There had been no rain for several weeks, and it was the work of a few minutes to slip down to the garden, take up a handful of soil and crumble it into the box. It looked so much like powder that Violet Elizabeth wondered whether a commercial enterprise on a large scale might be started later, when she had had time to think out the details. . . .

There remained the lipstick and the rouge. Patsy had taken the lipstick only, leaving the case intact. A crayon, thought Violet Elizabeth, would fit it nicely. . . . A red crayon, of course, for preference. Back in her bedroom, Violet Elizabeth hunted through her box of crayons. The red one would not fit. There was a blue one that fitted perfectly. Violet Elizabeth slipped it in and left it. She would cut down the red one to fit it later. There would be plenty of time. Probably her mother wouldn't look at the case for months. . . . Next, the rouge pot must be filled with red paint. Probably rouge was just red paint, anyway.

Violet Elizabeth took her paint box from her toy cupboard and examined it. The red paint was nearly finished, but there were full tubes of green, white, and cobalt blue. Violet Elizabeth was growing tired of the process of replenishing the case, and sounds of the arrival of the visitor downstairs warned her that it was nearly lunch time. After all, if the whole point of the process was to make it appear that mistakes had been made by the manufacturers, they might as well be real mistakes. She squeezed the tube of green paint into the rouge pot, screwed the top on firmly, then, as the luncheon bell sounded, slipped the case into its usual place on a shelf of her mother's wardrobe and went demurely down to the dining-room.

Mrs. Sedley-Mortimer was a small slight woman, so full of vitality that she seemed to quiver from head to foot even when standing or sitting quite still. She had untidy grey hair, sharp features, and an earnest expression, alternated by a flashing smile that came and went so quickly that one doubted its ever having come at all. Her chief characteristic was a capacity for talking incessantly without need of encouragement or response from her hearers, and she prided herself, rightly, on never being at a loss for a word. She said that from her earliest youth she had felt that her great gifts should be put at the service of her fellow creatures, and so she had put them at the service of her fellow creatures. Whether her fellow creatures appreciated them or not was a matter of indifference to her. She knew what was good for people, and she gave it them unstintingly, whether they wanted it or not. In her lightning tour of Southern England, she had left in her wake countless dispirited little branches of the Youth on the Prow Movement, led by local helpers after her own pattern, and she would pounce down upon each at regular intervals to "encourage and inspire" them, as she put it, leaving them even more dispirited than before. Mrs. Bott herself, who could hold her own with most people, was shattered by the full blast of Mrs. Sedley-Mortimer's eloquence. She couldn't get a word in edgeways. This increased her already deep respect for the lady and made her feel all the more flattered at having been chosen to co-operate with her.

Violet Elizabeth ate her lunch in silence—not from choice, but because anyone who lunched with Mrs. Sedley-Mortimer lunched perforce in silence, except, of course, for the insistent flow of Mrs. Sedley-Mortimer's bright incisive voice.

"I feel that I have a Call to this work," said Mrs. Sedley-Mortimer. "I feel that Youth needs a champion to assist it to fight those forces of self-indulgence and lack of restraint that are ranged against it to-day. I am convinced that——"

"Pleathe," piped Violet Elizabeth.

Violet Elizabeth had never intended to go to Mrs. Sedley-Mortimer's meeting, but had reserved her trump card for the last minute.

"Yes, dear," said Mrs. Bott, glad of the chance of hearing herself speak.

"Pleathe, I feel thick," said Violet Elizabeth.

Mrs. Bott looked at her in motherly consternation.

"You'd better go and have a lay-down, love," she said.

Mrs. Sedley-Mortimer watched Violet Elizabeth depart.

"An intelligent child," she said mechanically, for she knew that to its parents every child is intelligent, and that a good meal, especially in war-time, must be paid for in such coin.

"Well——" began Mrs. Bott, with a modest deprecating smile, but Mrs. Sedley-Mortimer, who, having paid her due to hospitality, considered the subject closed, cut in sharply.

"To begin with, I concentrate upon the girls, and I inaugurate my campaign by combating the immoderate use of cosmetics that is such a feature of the present day. I try to impress upon them that the process does not improve their appearance but, on the contrary, has a definitely disfiguring effect. It has been my custom to bring some cosmetics myself on to the platform and apply them to my face in order to prove my point, and to demonstrate the fact that they do not beautify a face but rob it of character and personality and, in a word, vulgarise it. I tell them that I shall not be satisfied till every girl and woman in England is going about undaubed and unpainted, as her Creator made her. . . . By the way, I have forgotten to bring my cosmetics for what I call my Object Lesson. I don't know whether you——?"

"Yes," admitted Mrs. Bott. "I can let you 'ave some. I don't use 'em much myself. Just a touch-up now and then. I don't see that young girls 'ave any call to use 'em. I'm with you there, all right. But us older ones——"

"Quite," said Mrs. Sedley-Mortimer tactfully. "It's young girls, of course, that I am chiefly concerned with. If you can kindly lend me——?"

"Oh, yes," said Mrs. Bott. "I've got some in a case that I only use to go away with. It'll be nice and 'andy for you to carry down to the Village 'All."

"Thank you," said the visitor. "And now perhaps I'd better start."

"I'm afraid I can't come to the meeting myself," said Mrs. Bott. "I'm not feelin' too grand, an' I might 'ave a turn any minute. I think I'd better go and 'ave a bit of a lay-down."

Though her respect for her visitor was still unbounded, she felt that she needed a little respite from her, even if it meant foregoing the meeting with the bishop. . . .

"Quite," said Mrs. Sedley-Mortimer, who didn't care whether Mrs. Bott went to her meeting or not, and had already told the Vicar not to come, as she established contact more easily if no other grown-ups were present. "If you'll just let me have this case."

"I'll get it," said Mrs. Bott.

Mrs. Sedley-Mortimer leapt brightly upon the platform, flashed the vanishing smile round the rows of gloomy young faces before her, and plunged straight into the heart of her discourse.

. . . "And, children, we have to *work* together, you and I. We have to *improve* ourselves and those around us, to make ourselves fit citizens of the New World that is coming. And I am here to help you to do this. I'll begin with you girls. . . . I want you first of all to promise me never to paint and daub your faces like savages, as so many girls do. You see them everywhere—and horrible sights they are, you will agree. Like beasts of prey, with their reddened mouths and nails. They only do it because other people do it. If we all band ourselves together to give up this horrible practice, it will cease. What I want you to realise this afternoon is that it is a definitely disfiguring process. It does not impart beauty. On the contrary. Moreover, it takes away all character from the face. And it is, of course, dishonest. It is Acting a Lie. Always remember that, girls. Acting a Lie. . . . Now I am going to give you an Object Lesson. Look at me carefully, children. I am not,

"YOU MAY WELL LAUGH," SAID
MRS. SEDLEY-MORTIMER.

of course, beautiful"—Mrs. Sedley-Mortimer laughed
gaily—"but there is, I think I may claim, a certain
character in my face. It has individuality. It has
truth. It is not a mere replica of a daubed and painted
mask. Now watch me very closely, children, while I
apply the disfiguring *coating* that you see around you
every day." She opened the pigskin case, took out a
jar, and read the inscription on the label: Vanishing
Cream. "This," she said brightly, "is what, I believe,
is applied first." With a lightning movement, she
dipped her finger into the red tile polish and smeared
it over her face. A titter arose. "Don't laugh too
soon," said Mrs. Sedley-Mortimer, "I'm going to be
much funnier before I've finished. . . . Rouge next,

I believe." She took up the jar labelled Rouge, opened it, and, without looking at its contents, her eyes still fixed on the rows of brightening faces, dipped a finger in the green paint and smeared it lavishly over both cheek-bones. The titter increased.

"Ah, you may laugh," said Mrs. Sedley-Mortimer. "You may well laugh. Doubtless I perform the process inexpertly, but, believe me, it is no funnier than what you see around you every day. It is a ridiculous custom, and my object is to make you see how ridiculous it is. So laugh as much as you like. Powder next, I believe." She opened the powder-box, and, taking a powder-puff from a compartment of the case, proceeded to apply a covering of garden soil to the green paint and tile polish. A roar of laughter arose.

"Wait for the lipstick," she said, delighted by her reception. (The Object Lesson had, she thought, never gone so well). "The lipstick completes the whole ridiculous effect." She drew the blue crayon carefully over her lips, her eyes still fixed on her rocking audience. "And if ever you are tempted to follow the foolish example set you by your elder sisters, remember this afternoon and say to yourselves: 'We laughed at Mrs. Sedley-Mortimer, and I shall look just as silly.' And now consider my face, children. Has it more character or less, more individuality or less, than when I started the revolting process?" Roars of laughter answered her. "Am I Acting a Lie or am I not?" Cheers answered her. "Now a word to you boys. Do you feel any greater respect for me than when I started to *daub* my face?" Mingled cries of "Yes" and "No," both drowned by shouting, laughing, cheering. Mrs.

Sedley-Mortimer flattered herself that she had brought home her point with even more vigour than usual. It was, she thought, a good note on which to end her address. "And now, children, that will be all for to-day. You have had an Object Lesson, which, I hope, you will remember for the rest of your lives." The uproarious response of the delighted children assured her that they would. "And next week we will start working really hard."

She sped (Mrs. Sedley-Mortimer never walked like other people) out of the Village Hall, still accompanied by the cheering children, down the road, up the Vicarage drive, and through the open french window into the Vicarage drawing-room, where the Vicar, the Vicar's wife, the Bishop, the Bishop's wife and a few of the more earnest-minded local inhabitants were waiting to welcome the Uplifter of Youth and to feed her on a war-time Vicarage repast of straw-coloured tea and butterless scones.

The Vicar's wife was ready to step forward and greet her, the Bishop's wife was ready to clasp her warmly by the hand and urge her not to flag in the noble work, however unresponsive her youthful audience might have shown itself. . . . But both remained motionless and speechless, petrified by amazement as the strange figure pranced in at the open window. The Vicar's wife blenched, and the Bishop's wife gave a strangled scream. The Bishop took off his spectacles and put them on again, somewhat surprised to find the vision still there at the end of the process. . . . The Vicar's expression grew stern as he faced the dreadful possibility that the woman Drank. The earnest-minded inhabitants drew together like a little

flock of sheep before a marauding wolf. Mrs. Sedley-
Mortimer remained blissfully unconscious of the consternation she was causing in the peaceful Vicarage
drawing-room. Mrs. Sedley-Mortimer was always
blissfully unconscious of everything except herself and
her Call.

"Delighted to meet all you good people," she said
brightly, flashing the vanishing smile round the room.
"Now don't let's bother with introductions because
names mean nothing to me, and I always forget them.
We are the Friends of Youth, and that is all that
matters. Dear Vicar, I hope to achieve great things
among the young people of your parish. Dear Bishop,
delighted to see you and your good lady—united with
us here in the Good Work. My little effort this afternoon will, I hope, bear fruit, will contribute its mite
towards building up a race of healthy-minded men
and women for the New World. I think that——"

The Vicar's wife suddenly found her voice.

"Wouldn't you like to have a wash, Mrs. Sedley-
Mortimer?" she said hysterically.

Mrs. Sedley-Mortimer's gay laugh rang out.

"You mean the daubs I have put upon my face?"
she said. "No, I shall keep them on. They have
served already as an Object Lesson, and even on the
way home they may still serve as an Object Lesson.
If people think how ridiculous I look, that is all I
require. It makes them laugh, but it makes them
think. The dear children laughed this afternoon, but
I'm sure they *thought*, too. . . ."

The Vicarage maid entered with the tea-pot and
looked at Mrs. Sedley-Mortimer with mild interest.
Crackers, of course, she thought, but they're all

EVERYONE WAS PETRIFIED AS THE STRANGE FIGURE
PRANCED IN.

crackers. I bet she's not worse than the rest. . . .
Stolidly she set down the tea-pot and departed. With
trembling hands the Vicar's wife poured out the tea.
Gazing at her intently (he couldn't decide what stage
of intoxication she had reached and whether it would
be wise to get in touch with the police), the Vicar
handed her her cup. Brightly, gaily, Mrs. Sedley-
Mortimer continued her monologue.

"So, if you think I look ridiculous, remember it's
all in a good cause, all for the foundation of a new and
better world." She glanced at her watch. "And now
I must fly, fly, fly to carry on the good work elsewhere.
I'll come over for the next meeting, dear Vicar, if
you'll let me know when it is. We must keep the
good work going, mustn't we? and not turn back
from the plough. So good-bye, all you dear people.
So sorry I can't stay longer, but time and tide, you
know. Or I might say, time-tables and trains. . . .
No, I don't want anyone to see me off. I am a walking
Object Lesson this afternoon and I shall try to improve
the occasion with anyone I meet who seems to look
at me with interest. I shall say: 'I am not myself.
My face is Telling a Lie. I am *daubed*—the character
of my face destroyed and *paint* put in its place.' Once
more, good-bye, good-bye. . . ."

Waving her hand to them, she flitted out of the
french window and vanished down the drive. For a
full minute no one spoke. When they did they all
spoke at once.

"A victim of the Bottle, I am afraid," said the
Vicar, shaking his head.

"Mad," said the Vicar's wife. "Stark, staring."

"Nothing would induce me now to associate myself

with her Movement," said Miss Milton with a shudder.

"Surely," said the Bishop in grim displeasure, "*surely* that—that *clown* is not the Mrs. Sedley-Mortimer you asked me here to meet?"

"I am afraid so, my lord," said the Vicar. "I am sadly afraid so. I had no idea, of course, of the woman's Weakness. We have seen her at an unfortunate moment——"

"More than unfortunate," said the Bishop.

"I agree, my lord. More than unfortunate. I need hardly say that I can no longer lend my countenance to the Movement she represents."

"But we must be *just*," said Mrs. Monks. "We were not at the meeting. We cannot know all the circumstances. There may be some explanation if——"

The Bishop raised an expostulatory hand.

"My dear lady, whatever the circumstances, whatever the explanation, whatever the excuse, the Movement cannot be allowed to function in this neighbourhood after this afternoon's indecorous exhibition."

"Quite," said the Vicar. "Quite."

Violet Elizabeth met William and Ginger in the old barn that evening.

"Why didn't you come to the meeting?" said William.

"I wath pretending to be thick," said Violet Elizabeth simply. "Wath it awful?"

"No, it was fun," said William. "You missed a jolly good time, didn't she, Ginger?"

"Yes, you did," said Ginger. "She was dull at first, then she did a sort of funny turn. Started putting

A THOUGHTFUL LOOK CAME INTO VIOLET ELIZABETH'S
FACE.

green paint and earth all over her face. Coo, she did
look funny!"

A thoughtful look came into Violet Elizabeth's face.
Green paint and earth. . . . She had not heard of the
borrowing of her mother's cosmetic case and she had
not been there when a small messenger brought it
back from the Village Hall with Mrs. Sedley-Mortimer's
compliments and thanks, to be returned by Mrs. Bott
to its place in her wardrobe without further investiga-
tion; but green paint and earth. . . .

"Come on. Let's go to the woods," said William.
"An' we don't want *you*," he added, turning to Violet
Elizabeth.

"An' I don't want *you*," countered Violet Elizabeth with spirit, "but you can't thtop me goin' to the woodth if I want to. It'th a free country, ithn't it?"

This interchange was merely formal. They all knew that Violet Elizabeth would accompany them to the woods and that nothing they could say or do would stop her.

They scrambled over the wooden railings and walked down the shady path beneath the trees. Suddenly William chuckled.

"She was *jolly* funny, wasn't she, Ginger?" he said. "Putting the blue crayon on her lips. . . ."

"Blue crayon, did you thay?" said Violet Elizabeth.

"Yes."

Suddenly, turning a bend in the path, they met Patsy and her young man. Patsy looked enchanting, with delicately rouged cheeks and a glowing cupid's bow of a mouth. The young man evidently thought so, too. He did not trouble to withdraw his arm as they approached. Patsy gave them a ravishing smile, followed by an almost imperceptible wink, and introduced them to him as her greatest friends. The young man, not wanting to waste time on them, greeted them heartily, gave them half a crown, and passed on. They stood and gazed after the couple.

"She looked jolly pretty," said William.

"Yes," agreed Ginger. "A bit different from that ole Mrs. What's-her-name."

The two boys laughed uproariously at the memory, but, as Violet Elizabeth walked on beside them, her face still wore that thoughtful look. . . .

CHAPTER X

AUNT FLORENCE, TOY MAKER

"IT'S a long time since we did anything about the war," said William.

"They won't *let* us do anything," grumbled Ginger. "We've tried often enough."

"No, but we haven't collected money for anything for ages."

"We tried collectin' salvage an' it didn't come off."

"No, but I mean *money*. We've gotter c'lect money for somethin', same as everyone else. Prisoners of War or somethin'."

"We never have any money."

"No, but we can make a *neffort*, can't we, same as they do an' raise some. They raise no end with Bring an' Buy sales an' suchlike."

"We've got nothin' to bring an' buy."

"I bet we could have if we had a look round. Toys an' things. Tell you what! We could have a Toy Bring an' Buy Sale. I bet we'd make a lot of money that way."

"We could try," said Ginger doubtfully.

So they tried. They put up a notice on the door of the old barn:

"A Bring and By Toy Sail will be held here in ade of the Prisoners of War next Satday. Pleese bring your toys and by your frends."

Things had been dull in the village lately, and, rather to the Outlaws' surprise, the youthful members of the community seized eagerly on the idea. There were animated discussions on every side as to what they would bring and what they would buy.

"If I bring that wooden engine of mine, can I buy your bucket an' spade?"

"Are you bringin' your scooter? I'll buy it if you are."

"What about your wheelbarrow? Are you bringin' it?"

Complicated "deals," worthy of the Stock Exchange, were transacted during History or Geography lessons.

"If I buy her tunnel an' you buy her station, I bet we can swop them for his set of soldiers."

Big Business invaded kindergarten and nursery. High Finance hovered round tousled heads and jammy mouths. . . . William was a little disconcerted by the enthusiasm his scheme had aroused.

"Gosh!" he said. "The whole lot of 'em's comin'. I bet it'll be an awful mess-up. It always is when the whole lot of 'em comes."

He asked his mother's advice on the organisation of a Bring and Buy Sale, but his mother's energies were absorbed in her own immediate war-time problems, and she took little interest in the affair.

"Well, they just come and—bring and buy, dear," she said. "That's all. There's nothing to worry about."

But it happened that Aunt Florence was paying a visit to William's home, and she took a keen interest in his Sale. It happened, too, that Aunt Florence had just purchased a book on toy making and was engaged in the making of a toy.

"It seems so simple, dear," she said. "I'd no idea how simple it was till I read the directions. You just knit the—the covering of the animal, as it were, then stuff it with something, and—there it is. Of course, one's a bit limited as to colour because one must just use whatever colour of wool one happens to have by one, and, of course, it may not be the natural colour of the animal, so to speak, but, after all, one must use one's imagination a little. Why else is it given us? I'll make a point of finishing this one by Saturday, dear boy, so that you can have it for your Sale. And

"I'LL FINISH IT BY SATURDAY," PROMISED
AUNT FLORENCE.

I'll come and help you. . . .   I'm a bit shaky on change, of course, but we'll manage all right."

Even William felt a little doubtful about Aunt Florence's "help". Aunt Florence was the vaguest person he had ever known. She set out for the post office and ended up at the butcher's. She went down to the library in Hadley to change her book several days running and each time forgot to take her book with her. She handed the bus conductor her ration book instead of her twopence. She went to church at eleven o'clock on Saturday and couldn't think why they weren't having Matins as usual. She left her things everywhere. She never knew where anything was. She sent people birthday cards at Christmas and Christmas cards on their birthdays. She wore her hats back to front and the wrong coats with the wrong skirts. . . .

But it was in her knitting that you saw the full fine flower of her vagueness. She began vests and they turned into scarves. She began scarves and they turned into bed jackets. She began with seventy stitches and in a few rows, for no apparent reason, they had doubled or halved themselves. She dropped stitches wildly and forgot to pick them up. . . . And none of this worried her. She knitted on and on with gay insouciance, perfectly satisfied with whatever form her knitting finally took. . . . And so the Brown family watched her "toy making" with awe and suspense. Only Aunt Florence seemed to be troubled by no doubts. She knitted on and on, mixing purl and plain, finding herself knitting on the wrong side and hastily turning back on her tracks, finding herself with forty stitches where she ought to have had thirty, dropping ten stitches to make it right, and "catching them up" with white cotton. She worked with a peculiar stitch —very large and loose, so that each stitch was apt to look like a hole. At intervals she would hold up the shapeless piece of knitting and view it undismayed.

"Of course," she would say, "till the stuffing's actually in, you can't see the real shape of the animal. I've got some cotton-wool to stuff it with, and I can't help thinking that it will look rather sweet. I shall love to think of some dear little soul cuddling it in bed at night. . . ."

William hoped that she would not have finished it by the day of the Sale. Certainly, when he went to bed the evening before, it was still a strange shapeless object, more suggestive of an antimacassar than anything else. But evidently Aunt Florence sat up over it late into the night, for she greeted him in the morning with shining eyes and a smile of proud achievement.

"Here it is, dear boy," she said, handing him a parcel done up in tissue paper. "All ready for your Sale and for some dear little soul to cuddle in bed at night."

William undid the parcel and looked at the shapeless repulsive object. So inadequate was the stuffing that it sagged in every direction. There were small appendages evidently meant to be legs, but no stuffing had found its way into them. There appeared to be no head, and only a couple of boot buttons (intended, one guessed, for eyes) distinguished the front of the creature from the rear. In whatever manner one picked it up, it hung in a limp bunch. Its colour was a peculiarly repellant shade of green, and the stuffing oozed freely through the large uneven stitches.

"It's *rather* attractive, isn't it?" said Aunt Florence

fondly. "Really, it was all I could do last night not
to take it to bed myself." It was clear that she saw
no flaw in her handiwork. "Sell it or raffle it, dear
boy. So long as the Prisoners of War reap the benefit
and some dear little soul cuddles it in bed at nights,
I shall consider my labour well rewarded."

William tucked it under one arm and a cardboard
box (in which to put the proceeds of the sale) under the
other, and set off for the old barn. The one bright
spot in the prospect was that Aunt Florence had a
slight cold and so could not come and "help." The
other Outlaws were there when he arrived and had
arranged a row of packing-cases to form a counter.
The customers, too, were already appearing—a tense
and anxious little crowd, with teddy bears, dolls, boxes
of bricks, toy engines, Noah's arks under their arms,
dragging scooters, toy carts, wheelbarrows. . . . From
the beginning, of course, the affair got out of hand.
Quarrels, disputes, bloody combats arose on all sides.
Screams of pain and anger rent the air.

"You promised it *me*!"

"I got hold of it first!"

"It's broken. You never told me it was broken, you
beastly old cheat!"

"I want it. I *told* you I wanted it."

Goods passed from hand to hand at prices arranged
by the parties themselves, instead of being given to the
Outlaws and set out on the counter. The Outlaws
stood helplessly by, realising the futility of doing anything else. Already William had had his nose punched
for trying to intervene between two boys who were
fighting—to the death, as it seemed—over a Hornby
train. Already Ginger had had his finger bitten by a

little girl, whom he was trying to save from murder at the hands of another little girl, who wanted the same doll. Yet, in spite of this seeming chaos, the cardboard box was gradually being filled. Parents and aunts had risen generously to the occasion. Hot little hands threw pennies, sixpences, shillings, even half-crowns into the box, while tense little voices panted: "That's

for his airgun," or "That's for her gollywog," before
the combatants flung themselves again madly into the
fray. As the first fury died down, some toys were
brought by newcomers, put on the counter, priced by
the Outlaws, and sold in a regular, orderly fashion,
vanishing almost as soon as they appeared. Only Aunt
Florence's toy remained—sprawled, shapeless, unsold,
unsaleable . . .

William did his best.

"Wouldn't you like to buy this?" he would say

"WHAT IS IT?" ASKED THE LITTLE GIRL.

G

persuasively, and the customer would eye it contemptuously and reply: "No fear!"

"It's very cheap," William would say, and "It'd need to be," would be the rejoinder.

"What is it?" said one little girl, looking at it curiously.

"A toy animal," said William.

"But *what* animal?" said the little girl.

William looked at it, baffled. Long, green, shapeless. . . . It might have been a snake or a caterpillar. . . . On the other hand, there were those four little appendages, obviously meant to be legs. Then William had a brain wave. He tore the fly-leaf out of a book of nursery rhymes that was hanging fire, and, writing on it: "THE GREEN MISTRY. WOT IS IT? PENNY A GESS. PRIZE TO WINER", propped it up against Aunt Florence's toy. Ginger ran home to fetch some paper (he was fortunate enough to find his mother's bureau open and his mother away) and the Outlaws tore it into small tickets. Customers crowded round to see what was happening. The idea caught on, and the counter was besieged. Ginger, Henry and Douglas formed the customers into a queue that discussed the problem with eager interest.

"I think it's a dragon."

"It might be a lizard."

"What about a whale?"

The pile of pennies grew, the last ticket was filled in . . . and the whole room gazed expectantly at William.

"Well, what *is* it?"

"I—I dunno," admitted William.

A murmur of disapprobation arose.

"I'll go'n' find out," said William. "I won't be a minute."

He ran home as quickly as he could. Aunt Florence was sitting by the window, doing some crochet work. Seen from the distance, she resembled a fisherman mending his nets.

"Well, dear boy," she said, looking up with a smile. "How is the Sale going?"

"Jolly well," said William.

"Has my animal sold yet?"

"They're jolly int'rested in it," said William. He looked at her, summoning all his (not very plentiful) resources of tact. "They want to know its name."

"Do they?" said Aunt Florence, pleased.

"They wondered whether to call it Pussy," said William, taking the bull by the horns.

"Oh, no," said Aunt Florence. "I don't think you could call a camel Pussy. I'd thought of——"

But William was already half-way back to the old barn.

"It's a camel," he said breathlessly as he entered.

A chorus of groans greeted him. No one had guessed a camel.

"Well, no one guessed right, so it all goes to the Prisoners of War," said William, pouring the pile of coppers into the cardboard box.

At that moment, Mrs. Monks, the Vicar's wife, entered.

"I've only just heard of your little effort, children," she said. "Most commendable, but you should have told me. You should have asked me to help. I should have been only too glad to——" Her eyes fell upon Aunt Florence's toy. "What on earth's that?"

"A toy," explained William. "A home-made toy. It's a camel."

The Vicar's wife's eyes gleamed.

"Is it sold?"

"No."

"Then I must buy it. It's just what I want for my lecture on toy making to the Women's Institute. How much is it? One shilling? Two? . . . Here's half a crown. All in a good cause. And I'm very glad to have it."

She tucked the camel under her arm, patted such small heads as could not get out of her way in time, murmured absent-mindedly to a teddy bear that she hoped to see him in Sunday School next Sunday and drifted off.

William, accompanied by the Outlaws and a jostling scuffling crowd of customers, still disputing possession of treasured toys and literally "fighting their battles o'er again," made his way to the house of the local Red Cross Secretary and handed in his cardboard box. The Secretary was surprised and gratified by the result, congratulated William, shook hands with him, looked disapprovingly at the customers and begged them to remember that they were little ladies and gentlemen, not little savages, gave William a receipt (much to William's bewilderment, who had never seen one before), dodged a badly aimed clod of earth hurled by the indignant purchaser of a silent whistle at its original owner, closed the door hastily and retired.

William set out for home, the band of customers dropping off one by one as they approached their own homes, till a small child, howling loudly and demanding its sixpence back because its toy soldier wouldn't stand

THE SECRETARY CONGRATULATED WILLIAM AND SHOOK
HANDS WITH HIM.

up, was his only escort. William shut the door firmly
in its face and entered the morning-room, where Aunt
Florence sat in a sea of crochet work.

"Did it sell, dear?" said Aunt Florence eagerly.

"Oh, yes," said William. "It sold all right. Mrs.
Monks bought it for her lecture on toy making at the
Women's Institute."

Aunt Florence's face shone.

"Isn't that lovely, dear boy? What an honour! Somehow I thought it was rather a success. It had such an endearing expression. *Most* encouraging. I shall certainly try another pattern now. By the way, I'd like to go to that lecture. I shall feel so proud to see my little effort used as an object lesson. When is it, do you know?"

"It's generally on Tuesday afternoon," said William. "Three o'clock, I believe."

"I'll be there," said Aunt Florence happily.

And she was there. The room was rather full and she could only just squeeze into the back row. People round her were talking, Aunt Florence was rather deaf, and Mrs. Monks had not a very penetrating voice. But she saw Mrs. Monks hold up the sagging green object, apparently pointing out its merits to her audience.

"This," Mrs. Monks was saying, "is a perfect example, ladies, of how *not* to make a toy. Every possible fault is exemplified in it, and I need hardly point them out in detail. Note the loose knitting, the dropped stitches, the inadequate stuffing, the constant mistakes. The result resembles no creature that ever existed in or out of Toyland."

And Aunt Florence, who couldn't hear a word, sat and beamed proudly in the back row. . . .

During the interval for tea, the committee of the Women's Institute conferred hastily over the little collection of toy animals that had been used as models by Mrs. Monks.

"We'll sell these for the W.I. funds," said Mrs. Monks. "I shan't be giving this lecture again."

"But what about this?" said someone, holding up Aunt Florence's toy. "No one will buy it."

Miss Milton looked at it with a keen and speculative eye.

"One minute," she said briskly. "I think I can deal with that. Has anyone a needle and thread?"

Mrs. Monks had a needle and thread, and Miss Milton set to work at once. In a masterly fashion she turned the "toy" back upon itself, stitched together what should have been its backbone, snipping off the boot buttons and concealing the embryonic legs.

"There!" she said triumphantly. "Not perfect, of course, even as a tea cosy, but definitely a tea cosy."

They gazed at it in admiration. It was definitely a tea cosy. Already Miss Milton was writing out its price card: "TEA COSY 2/6."

"Put them all out and the women can buy them after tea."

Aunt Florence arrived home that evening with a parcel under her arm.

"I've had such a nice afternoon," she said, "and I've bought a tea cosy. Pretty, isn't it?" she went on, unwrapping it and holding it up admiringly. "It's rather the same colour as my dear camel, but not quite, of course. My dear camel wasn't on sale. I suppose that Mrs. Monks is keeping it for her next lecture. *Such* a compliment!" She examined the tea cosy closely. "I really think I could make one. I must try. . . . Now that I have had such a success with my camel, I must be a little more ambitious. I have some yarn of a pretty grey shade that I could use for it. I must set to work to-morrow. It will just do for a friend whose birthday it is next week."

So next day Aunt Florence set to work. It was a

A STREAM OF VILLAGE CHILDREN PASSED THE WINDOW.

fine day, and she sat by the open window, knitting, as usual, wildly, erratically, but with a proud smile on her face, for she still felt uplifted by the success of her camel.

"I expect Mrs. Monks will use it for all her lectures on toy making," she murmured. "Most gratifying."

William, for his part, still felt uplifted by the success of his Bring and Buy Sale and was reluctant to consider

his effort at an end.   He wanted an idea for continuing
it, and the sight of Aunt Florence knitting at the open
window gave him his idea.

Aunt Florence saw him climbing up the trellis by the
window, but was too much absorbed in her task to do
more than murmur: "Be careful, dear boy." She
noticed a stream of village children passing the window
and gazing in at her.   To each she gave a pleasant
greeting, murmuring at intervals: "So nice and
friendly, these country children."

She did not know, of course, that above the open
window was fixed a notice: "WOT IS SHE NITTING
NOW? PENNY A GESS. PRIZE FOR WINER."
She did not know that the queue was controlled by
William at one end, collecting pennies and issuing
blank tickets, and by Ginger at the other, collecting
completed tickets.   Many and varied were the guesses,
including almost every animal under the sun, and the
grand total of three shillings was realised.

"None of you's right," said William triumphantly at
the end, "so it all goes to the Prisoners of War.   She's
making a tea cosy."

But William was wrong.

Aunt Florence's effort was stuffed and despatched to
her friend the next day, but it must have disintegrated
in the post, for Aunt Florence received a letter from
the recipient by return: "Thank you so much, dear, for
the dish-cloth—a most acceptable gift these days.   As
for the packing you sent it in, it will come in most
useful to stuff a toy I am making. . . ."

CHAPTER XI

FEASTS FOR HEROES

"ANYWAY, this little girl told me all about it," said Henry. "She said that her father was goin' up to London to be decorated by the King this morning, an' her mother an' her were goin' with him, an' they'd be back for tea, an' that the aunt what was goin' to come an' get their tea ready for them was ill an' couldn't, an' I think it's jolly hard lines on them comin' back from bein' decorated by the King an' havin' to get their own tea."

"Where do they live?"

"In the new estate at Marleigh. Her father's at Marleigh Aerodrome, an' they've only jus' come there, an' they don't know anyone yet, so they can't get anyone else to get their tea. Well, I think it's jolly hard lines to come back from bein' decorated by the King, and have to get their own tea."

"What house do they live at? It's full of houses."

Henry considered.

"Well, she told me. I don't quite remember. It was somethin' to do with a sort of tree. I know! It was The Lilacs or The Laburnums, or somethin' like that. I know her name was Ann. Anyway, I think it's jolly hard lines to come back from bein' decorated by the King an' to have to——"

"Oh, shut up sayin' that," said William irritably. "*Course* it is, but it's no good keepin' on *sayin'* it."

"Couldn't we *do* somethin'?" said Douglas.

"Course we could," said William, "but we've gotter think it out a bit first . . . Let's go 'n' find the house."

They collected Ginger and Douglas, and the four of them set off for the Marleigh estate. There they paused, disconcerted, looking round at the warren of small roads that confronted them—Pine Avenue, Forest Glade, The Glen, Fir Tree Road. . . .

"Didn't she say the name of the road?" said William.

"N-no, she jus' said The Lilacs or The Laburnums or whatever it was. I *think* it was The Lilacs. Or it may've been The Laburnums."

"Gosh!" said William severely. "Fancy not gettin' to know a bit more than that!"

"Well, she was called Ann."

"*That's* not much help . . . Well, come on. We'll have to go round the whole place till we find it."

An exhaustive search of Pine Avenue, Forest Glade and The Glen revealed no more arboreous names than The Firs, The Laurels and Beech View.

"No, it wasn't any of them," said Henry firmly. "It was somethin' with a flower on it, like The Lilacs or The Laburnums. I think it was The Lilacs. If it wasn't, it was The Laburnums."

Half-way up Fir Tree Road Ginger, who had run on ahead, gave a shout of excitement.

"Here it is!" he said. "I've got it—The Lilacs!"

"Yes, it *was* 'The Lilacs,'" said Henry. "I remember now. It *was* The Lilacs."

They clustered round the gate, looking up at the little house.

"Don't see any lilac," objected Douglas.

"That doesn't matter, you idiot! The Lilacs is jus' its name. There wasn't any firs in The Firs, an' I couldn't see a beech from Beech View. It's jus' its *name*."

"P'raps they planted one an' it died," suggested Henry.

"Anyway, I'm goin' to see if anyone's in," said William. "I'm goin' to knock at the door."

"What'll you do if someone comes?"

"I'll ask if Mr. Jones lives there," said William promptly. "I always do that if I want to find out if anyone's in a house."

"S'pose Mr. Jones *does* live there?"

"He never has yet. I'll think up somethin' quick if he does."

He walked up to the front door and knocked loudly. The three Outlaws at the gate stood poised for instant flight. William practised the bland expression with which he was wont to ask for Mr. Jones. . . . There was no answer. William knocked again. There was still no answer. Dismissing the bland expression, he turned to his accomplices.

"Come on," he said shortly. "Let's go round to the back."

They went round to the back and knocked at the back door.

"We'll say we're collectin' salvage if anyone comes," said William. "It's best to keep Mr. Jones for front doors."

But still no one answered the knock.

"They're out," deduced William with a thoughtful frown.

"Course they are," said Henry. "I told you

they were, didn't I? They've gone to London to be decorated by the King. An' I think it's jolly hard lines to come home from bein' decorated by the King an' have to get your own tea."

"Shut *up* sayin' that," said William. "Anyway, we're doin' all we can, aren't we?"

"We've not done much so far."

"Well, we've not *started* yet. Gimme time to *think* . . . I'm goin' to try the window."

"COURSE THEY'RE OUT," SAID HENRY.
"I TOLD YOU THEY WERE."

He tried the window. It slid up easily. One after another, the Outlaws climbed through into the little kitchen. It was neat and spotless, but there were no traces of preparation for a meal. The dining-room was also neat and spotless, but the table was not even laid.

"They've gotter start right from the beginnin' when they come in," said Henry gloomily. "Right from puttin' the kettle on an' settin' the table an' gettin' the bread out."

Ginger was inspecting the larder.

"There's no food at all," he said in horrified tones. "Gosh! I dunno what they're goin' to eat. Jus' a loaf an' a bottle of milk an' a tiny bit of butter. Gosh! That's not much of a tea to come home to after bein' decorated by the King."

"It's 'cause of this aunt bein' ill," said Henry. "She was goin' to come an' get their tea."

"Well, now we're here," said Douglas, "what're we goin' to do?"

"We've gotter get'em a proper tea," said William firmly. "We can't let'em come home to this."

"Not after bein' decorated by the King," said Henry.

"Yes, we've jolly well got to," said Ginger. "A hero like that! After all he's done for the country—whatever it is an' I bet it's somethin' jolly brave—we can't let him come home to bread an' butter. An' I bet it was marge at that. No, we've gotter pay him back a bit for all he's done for us."

They were rapt with patriotic fervour till Douglas brought them down to earth by saying:

"How're we goin' to do it?"

"Well, I s'pose we can each go home an' get somethin'."

There was a depressed silence during which a mental vision of the state of his home larder came to each Outlaw.

"I bet I couldn't find anythin' much better than what they've got here," said William at last. "We only have cake on Tuesday, an' it's all et up by Wednesday."

"We had some biscuits las' week-end," said Henry, "but they're finished now an' we haven't any more points."

"My mother used our las' jelly for my birthday," said Douglas. "Gosh! I wish she hadn't."

"We haven't had any jelly for *years*," said Henry wistfully. "Fancy, when you could jus' go into shops an' buy 'em!"

"An' ice cream . . ." said Douglas. "Fancy, when you could jus' stop a man an' buy it!"

"An' bananas," said Henry. "Jus' go to a stall in the street an' buy *dozens!*"

"We're not talkin' about ice cream an' bananas," said William, sternly bringing them back to the business in hand. "We're talkin' about this tea an' how we're goin' to get it. Hasn't *anyone* got *anything?*"

"If it'd been the beginning of the month we'd've had some sweet coupons," said Henry.

"Well, it isn't, an' we haven't," said William shortly.

"Those las' mint balls I bought didn't taste of anythin'," said Douglas. "I wouldn't've minded a nasty taste, but they didn't taste of *anythin'!*"

William groaned.

"Can't anyone say anythin' sensible?" he said. "Here we are trespassin' in someone's house an' as like as not to be put in prison nex' minute, an' all you can do is to waste time talkin' about bananas an' mint balls."

They had not noticed the absence of Ginger, but suddenly he burst excitedly into the room.

"I say!" he said. "I've been havin' a look round, an' it's somebody's birthday down the road, an' they've got a scrumptious birthday tea ready an' gone out, an' I bet it's all right to take it for this man what's been decorated by the King. I bet no one's any right to have birthday teas like that while people what've been decorated by the King haven't got any tea at all."

"How d'you know it's their birthday?" said William.

"There's a birthday card on the table—I could see it through the window, an'—*Gosh!* It's a real birthday tea. There's iced cake an' chocolate biscuits an' ginger biscuits an' a jelly an' little cakes an' all sorts of sandwiches."

"Well, we can't jus' *steal* it," said Henry righteously.

"It's not stealin'," said William. "It's takin' it from people what don't need it an' oughtn't to have it to give it to people what do need it an' ought to have it. It's what Robin Hood did an' no one ever thinks it was wrong of him. There's plays an' poems wrote about him."

"Well, I bet if anyone catches us they won't write plays an' poems about *us*," said Henry.

"There's an awful long poem about Robin Hood," said Douglas. "We learnt it at school, an' I never could remember it."

"I saw a film about him once," said Ginger. "It was a jolly good film. There was a fat man in it called Friar Tuck, an' he made everyone roar with laughter. He——"

"I wish you'd stop *talkin'*," interrupted William. "We shall get put in prison before we've done *anythin'* at this rate. Here's this man been decorated by the King, an' comin' home an'——"

At this point Ginger, who as usual had not been wasting time, emerged from a small pantry with two large baskets.

"Look!" he said. "I've found these. They'll do to carry the stuff across in. It's only down at the end of the road. Better jus' two of us go an' the other two stay here an' set the stuff out when we bring it back. Come on, William. You an' me'll go."

The exploit was easier of achievement than they had expected. The scullery window was unlatched, and William climbed through and unlocked the kitchen door. They filled their baskets from the laden table, then returned to The Lilacs and, leaving the others to arrange the spoils, set off for the rest.

"We'll take the table-cloth, too," said William. "It's a jolly nice one, an' this man what's been decorated by the King's jolly well got a better right to it than this person what's only got a birthday . . . Let's be jolly careful with the jelly. Put it right on top an' walk as careful as you can."

Even the ticklish business of the jelly was accomplished without disaster. Though it wobbled precariously on the way, it arrived, shaken but intact, at its destination. They surveyed their handiwork with approval—the cloth of old gold damask, the jelly, the biscuits, the cake, the sandwiches.

"There's only some rotten utility cups an' saucers here," said Ginger. "There's some jolly nice ones at the other house. Let's fetch 'em. It seems jolly hard on a man what's been decorated by the King to have to drink his tea out of rotten utility cups an' saucers."

The other two demanded their fair share of excitement, so this time it was Henry and Douglas who set off with the baskets to fetch the crockery.

"I bet they'll make a mess of it," said William

"THEY SURVEYED THEIR HANDIWORK WITH APPROVAL."

gloomily. "They'll break it on the way, or get caught or somethin'."

But even this final tempting of providence passed off successfully, and in a few minutes they returned, their baskets filled with cups and saucers and plates not even cracked.

"We found a silver teapot, too," said Douglas, bringing out his trophy with an air of pride. "It's only right this man should have a silver teapot after bein' decorated by the King. This other person's got no right to it at all."

"I didn't think we oughter start takin' silver teapots," said Ginger apprehensively. "I don't think it's *right* takin' silver teapots."

"I bet Robin Hood wouldn't've stopped at a silver teapot," said Douglas. "I bet a silver teapot was nothin' to Robin Hood. I bet he took *hundreds* of 'em every day. Anyway, my mother's always sayin' to me that if a thing's worth doin' at all it's worth doin' well. An' it seems silly to give him all that nice food an' cups an' saucers an' things, an' not a silver teapot. I bet he'll be jolly glad to see it."

They set out the latest spoils then once more surveyed their handiwork with critical pride.

"Flowers!" said William suddenly. "We oughter have some flowers. People always have flowers for parties."

"There were some jolly fine flowers in this other garden," said Ginger, still consumed by the lust for adventure. "They were the best flowers I've ever seen, an' I bet this man's got a better right to them than anyone else. If a man what's done all

that for his country, whatever he's done, hasn't a
better right to a few flowers with his tea than a man
what's done nothin' at all . . ."

Before they knew what he was about he had vanished,
to reappear in a few minutes' time with an armful of
enormous chrysanthemums, each about the size of
his own head.

"They're bigger than what I thought they were,"
he said doubtfully. "I don't know but what they're
a bit too big."

"No, they're jus' right," William assured him.
"You can't give a man what's been decorated by the
King niggly little flowers. He deserves somethin'
big. Look! Here's an empty marmalade jar they can
go in."

"Shall I fetch a few chairs from the other place?"
said Ginger, who was longing to essay the perilous
journey once again. "There were some jolly fine
chairs there. An' there were some nice ornaments
on the mantelpiece, too."

"No," said William firmly. "We've got enough
stuff from there. . . . Well, what do we do next?"

"We've gotter meet his train," said Ginger. "The
aunt would've met his train. It'll be jolly dull for
him after doin' a brave deed like that an' bein' decorated by the King if no one meets his train." Again
he looked complacently at the table. "I bet it's as
good a tea as his aunt would have got."

"We ought to have Union Jacks," said William.

"Shall I go'n' see if I can find one in the other
house?" said Ginger hopefully.

"*No*," said William. "I've jus' told you we've got
enough stuff from the other house. Anyway, I think

there's one at home, left over from somethin' or other.
We can call for it on the way to the station."

"We don't know what time the train gets in."

"Well, there's the one that gets in at 5.30.   I 'spect
they'll come by that.   Most people do."

THEY STOOD IN A ROW, WITH SOLEMN FACES.

"We'd better hurry, then. I'll put the kettle on a low gas an' we can make the tea for them as soon as we get 'em in."

They called at William's house for the Union Jack—it was small and shabby and faded, but it was undoubtedly a Union Jack—then set off for the station, where they stood in a row with set solemn faces, William at the end, holding his Union Jack.

The London train drew in, and the passengers began to descend. From the second carriage descended a Flying Officer, with wings and a ribbon on his tunic, accompanied by a woman and a little girl. The little girl was small and compact with dark curly hair.

"Is that the one?" whispered William to Henry.

"Yes," said Henry with decision, then, with less decision: "Yes, I'm pretty sure it is."

William stepped forward, barring the man's way, his face set and scowling with the solemnity of the occasion.

"We've come to take you to your house," he said.

The man did not seem particularly surprised.

"Thanks so much," he said. "It's on the Estate, isn't it?"

"Yes," said William, thinking it natural enough that the exciting events of the day should have blurred the hero's memory even of where he lived, and added: "We've got tea for you."

"Very good of you," said the man, but again he did not seem particularly surprised or even grateful.

The procession set out. In front walked William and Ginger, William carrying his flag, next came the Flying Officer with his wife and little girl, while Henry and Douglas brought up the rear.

"Of course," said William, turning round, "people don't know about it or everyone'd've come to meet you."

At this the Flying Officer did look a little blank. All he said, however, was: "Why?"

"He's not goin' to talk about what he's done," said William to Ginger. "He's modest, same as all brave men. But I bet we'll get him to tell us about it while he's havin' tea."

They led the way to the Estate, down Fir Tree Road, and in at the front door of The Lilacs. William flung open the dining-room door.

"The kettle's boiling," he said. "We'll have the tea made in no time."

The man entered the dining-room and gaped in amazement.

"*Gosh!*" he said. "What a spread!"

"Well, you've deserved it," said William. "You've *jolly* well deserved it."

"I don't know how I've deserved it," said the man, but his voice was drowned by screams of delight from the little girl.

"Oh, Daddy! . . . *Jelly!* . . . Chocolate *biscuits!*"

His wife had at first been speechless with amazement. Now she sank down weakly on the nearest chair and said:

"Whoever's done this?"

"We have," said William complacently. "We wanted you to have a good tea."

"How—how kind of you!" she said faintly, looking more bewildered than ever.

"The tea's made," said Ginger, proudly carrying in the silver teapot.

"Oh, come on!" said the little girl excitedly. "Come on! Isn't it *lovely!*"

The woman gazed round at the laden table and the rather top-heavy chrysanthemums in the marmalade jar. . . .

"This—this is surely rather unusual, isn't it?" she said, still in that faint, far-away voice. "Or—is there no shortage of food in this district?"

"Oh, there's a shortage of food, all right," said William, cheerfully. "But—well, this is a special occasion."

"Is it?"

William gave her a conspiratorial wink as much as to say: "You know it is. You can't fool me."

Still looking somewhat dazed, the family sat down and started on the tea.

The four Outlaws hovered about the Flying Officer, hanging over his shoulder, breathing down his neck, passing him sandwiches, cake, biscuits, with embarrassing rapidity.

"We know you don't want to talk about it," said William. "We know they never do, but—do tell us—was it bombing Berlin?"

"What *are* you talking about?" said the man.

The Outlaws burst into a roar of delighted laughter.

"We *knew* you wouldn't," said William, "but we're jolly glad you got back safe from wherever it was."

At this point there was a knock at the front door, and the woman went to open it.

"May I use your telephone, please?" they heard a voice say breathlessly. "Yours seems to be the only one in the road, and it's *most* urgent."

"Certainly," said the Flying Officer's wife. "Come in. We've only just arrived, but—Oh, here it is, by the door."

She returned to the dining-room, leaving the door ajar, and soon the breathless voice was heard again from the hall.

"Is that the Police? . . . Will you come quickly, please, to The Laburnums, Fir Tree Road? . . . It's a burglary . . . Yes, a *burglary* . . . Someone's been and taken *everything* while my husband and I were out. . . . Well, *nearly* everything . . . *all* the crockery and a valuable Queen Anne teapot . . . and even some prize chrysanthemums out of the garden which don't belong to us. . . . I'm afraid it's a case of juvenile crime. The only clue we can find is a boy's school scarf with the name William Brown inside. It should be possible to trace the criminal through that, I should think. The amazing thing is that they've taken every *morsel* of food. You see, my husband's been up to Buckingham Palace for a decoration, and a friend of mine got the tea ready for us, but couldn't stay till we returned. I don't know what she left, but every crumb's gone—table-cloth and everything. Yes, will you come at once? . . . The Laburnums . . . Actually the name isn't on the gate—the plate's come off—but there's a laburnum in the garden, and it's the only one in the road. . . ."

There was the sound of the receiver being replaced, and a small red-haired woman appeared in the doorway.

"I'm so sorry to hear of your misfortune," said the Flying Officer's wife, adding hospitably: "Do have a cup of tea with us before you go."

But the red-haired lady stood petrified, her gaze

riveted on the table, while the colour slowly ebbed from her cheeks.

"So it's *you!*" she said fiercely, then went on with what was obviously a burst of inspiration: "I warn you that the house is surrounded, and that if anyone tries to escape they'll be shot."

She darted out and they heard her at the telephone again.

"The police? . . . Come at once to The Lilacs, Fir Tree Road. . . . I've got the whole gang of them here. They're desperate, and I can't hold them much longer unless my husband comes. . . . He may be coming any minute because he wanted to telephone you himself, but I thought there wasn't a moment to be lost. . . . Yes, please, come at once. . . . The Lilacs."

The Flying Officer and his wife gazed at each other blankly.

"What on earth is happening?" said the Flying Officer. "Is she crazy or are we or is everyone?" He turned to William. "Do you know anything about this?"

The Outlaws were staring at each other with open jaws and horror-stricken eyes. Then their gaze concentrated slowly, accusingly, on Henry.

"Well, I wasn't sure," he said, "but I *thought* it was The Lilacs."

Again they heard the voice in the hall.

"Oh, there you are, John. What a mercy you've come! Have you got your revolver? I've got the whole gang here, but I can't hold them much longer. They look pretty dangerous. They're in that room, *with* all the loot."

The door was flung open. A Squadron Leader

stood in the doorway. Beside him was a little girl with dark curly hair. At sight of each other the officers gave shouts of joyful recognition.

"Corky! Where on earth have you sprung from?"

"Just been posted here," said the Flying Officer," "but we seem to have landed in a luny bin. A friend of mine got us this house and said he'd send someone to show us the way to it, and get in a bite of food for us as he was on duty himself, but I never expected anything like this."

"I bet you didn't. Our cups and saucers and

teapot and all! Who are these boys, by the way?"

"Haven't the faintest. I took for granted that my friend had sent them to show us the way to the house, but I'm beginning to wonder . . ." He turned to William: "Who are you?"

WILLIAM'S EXPLANATION WAS LONG AND INVOLVED.

William gulped and swallowed.

"Well," he began, "it was like this . . ."

His explanation was long and involved. At the end the two families burst into roars of laughter, which were interrupted by a smart knocking at the front door.

"The police!" said everyone simultaneously.

"I'll deal with them," said the Squadron Leader.

He returned a few minutes later.

"I've dealt with them," he said. "I told them it was a misunderstanding. They took some disposing of, but I think I've disposed of them at last."

The little girls were already fraternising over the feast.

"I've not had chocolate biscuits since my birthday," said one.

"And I've not had jelly since Christmas," said the other.

"They—they *are* a bit alike," said Henry apologetically, watching them, "an' I *thought* it was The Lilacs."

"Yes, you messed it up nicely, didn't you?" said William bitterly.

"But I think it's lovely," said the red-haired woman. "Let's all sit down and start tea. It's a real party instead of only being the three of us. It's wonderful. It's my birthday, too, and I was longing for a party. . . . Come on, all of you! There's masses of food for everyone. Come on, you two!" For the men were still animatedly comparing experiences since their last meeting.

"Right!" said the Squadron Leader. "And our four hosts must certainly stay. Scurry round and find some more chairs."

They scurried round and found some more chairs.

Henry, before devoting himself to the feast, stammered out a few more apologies.

"That's all right," said the Squadron Leader. "All children of that age look exactly alike, and the best people confuse lilac and laburnum. I think you managed marvellously. Now set to, all of you."

"Please, sir," faltered William, "will you—will you tell us what you did? For the decoration, I mean."

"Certainly," said the Squadron Leader heartily.

An hour later the Outlaws, gorged and happy, started off for home.

"It was the best party I've ever been to," said Ginger. "Not jus' since the war, but ever."

"Yes, it jolly well was," agreed the others.

"I don't think he really got that decoration for what he said he did," said Henry slowly. "I don't think he really got it for rescuin' the general's pet monkey what had got captured by the Germans. He winked at the other man when he said it."

"P'raps not, but he made a jolly excitin' story of it."

William took out of his pocket one of the ginger biscuits that the Squadron Leader had lavishly showered upon them when they left, and began to munch it happily.

"An' he said we could go 'n' see him again tomorrow."

"Yes, we'll get him to tell us the Real Story then."

With thoughts hovering round past, present and future—the feast, the ginger biscuits, the Real Story— the Outlaws strolled blissfully homewards through the dusk.

CHAPTER XII

WILLIAM GOES FRUIT PICKING

"NOW remember, dear," said Mrs. Brown, "you mustn't eat a single one."

"'Course I won't," said William indignantly. "D'you think I'd hold up the nation's food supply like that? Ole Marky gave us a talk about it an' he said we were helpin' to solve the nation's food problem an' if we ate a single one what we weren't given we'd be robbin' poor housewives what wait in queues."

"Oh well, I'm glad he put it like that," said Mrs. Brown, hoping for the best. She examined her son critically. "You don't look very tidy."

"He told us to put on our oldest clothes."

"Well, you've certainly done that. . . . What are you going to pick?"

"Dunno. We're all meetin' at the station an' goin' by train to Applelea to this farm. Stinks is takin' us. He said he couldn't see us doin' any real work, but it'd keep us out of mischief."

"I hope so," sighed Mrs. Brown. Somehow she didn't think that even fruit picking could keep William out of mischief. . . . "You'll remember about not eating any, won't you, dear? Have you got your sandwiches? . . . That's right. What time is the train? Hadn't you better start?"

"It's at ten-forty. We're all meetin' at the station. Ginger's callin' for me. . . . Hello, Ginger!"

For at this moment Ginger had arrived breathless, in old corduroy shorts and a ragged jersey.

"Come on," he said. "Ole Stinks said we'd gotter be at the station by half-past."

"All right," said William easily. "There's heaps of time."

They sauntered down the road, discussing fruit picking as they went.

"Hope it's strawberries," said Ginger.

"I bet they wouldn't let us pick strawberries," said William. "Hope they don't, too. It'd be *jolly* hard not to eat strawberries. I mean, you jus' eat 'em without knowin' you've et 'em. . . ."

"What about raspberries?"

"They're almost as bad. I jolly well hope it isn't raspberries."

"Well, what do you hope it is, then?"

William considered.

"Gooseberries," he said at last. "I shouldn't mind gooseberries. You *can* pick gooseberries without eatin' 'em. If you don't start, I mean. They're the same as everythin' else in that way. Once you've started you can't stop."

Ginger agreed, and, having exhausted the subject of fruit picking, they turned their attention to their immediate surroundings.

"I bet you couldn't climb to the top of that tree."

"I bet I could."

"I bet you couldn't. *Or* the one nex' to it."

"That's easier."

"It isn't."

"It is."

"It isn't."

"It is."

"All right. You take the one you say's easier an'

н

I'll take the other an' we'll have a race. We've got
our tree climbin' things on an' it seems a pity to waste
'em. I bet I get to the top first.''

"All right. You go an' stand at the bottom of
your tree an' I'll stand at the bottom of mine an' we'll
say, 'One, two, three.'''

"You're not to use the gate.''

"No, an' you're not to use the fence.''

"All right. Now, come on! . . . Ready? . . .
One, two three, *go*!''

Both trees presented considerable difficulty, and
about five minutes had passed before—at the identical

TWO HEADS EMERGED FROM THE TOP BRANCHES.

moment—the two heads emerged from the leafy top branches.

"A draw," pronounced William judicially.

"Yes, a draw," agreed Ginger. "I bet they were jus' about as hard as each other. Mine's goin' to be jolly hard to get down."

"So's mine."

"Let's not race down. There's an old nest in mine I want to have a look at."

"Yes, an' there's a hole in mine I want to have a look at. Shouldn't be surprised if it's an owl's nest."

Their descent was a lengthy one, but finally they dropped—again at almost the same moment—from the lowest branch and rolled on to the grass within a few yards of each other.

"What sort of a nest was it?"

"I think it was a thrush's. Was your hole an owl's nest?"

"No, it was jus' an ordin'ry hole. I say, I could see right over to Marleigh from the top of mine."

"So could I from the top of mine."

"You look awful. There's more tears in your jersey."

"There's more in yours, too. An' your face is all dirty."

"So's yours."

"An' your hair's an awful mess."

"So's yours."

"It doesn't matter, anyway. They said come in ole clothes. . . . I say!" with sudden apprehension. "I wonder what time it is."

"Dunno. It can't be late. We started out jolly early. P'raps we won't be there by half-past, but I bet we catch the train all right."

"Come on. We'd better hurry." He began to run then stopped suddenly. *"Gosh!"*

"What?"

"He told us to bring baskets."

"Corks! I quite forgot. We'd better go back for 'em."

"We can't. We'd miss the train. . . . I say!" They were passing the gates of the Hall, and William looked speculatively at the imposing mansion that could be seen through the trees. "I wonder if Mrs. Bott'd lend 'em us. She would if she was in a good mood."

"Yes, an' she wouldn't if she wasn't. Anyway, we've not got time to go up all the drive an' knock at the door an' explain to her. Let's go to that shed by the stables an' see if we can find some. I bet she wouldn't mind us borrowing them to help solve the nation's food problem."

They went round to the shed, which contained an imposing array of gardening implements.

"Here's a basket" said Ginger. "Bags me this one! It's jus' an ordin'ry gardening one. It can't do it any harm."

"Here's another!" said William. "It's rather a swanky one, but it's got a bit of newspaper at the bottom, so it can't get spoilt. I bet she wouldn't mind us takin' them."

"Well, come on! It's gettin' later an' later. We'll miss the train if we're not quick. Let's run."

They ran down the road.

"'S all right," panted Ginger, as they rounded the bend that led to the station. "The train's still in. We'll catch it. . . ."

Down the road, in at the station gate and on to the platform, just as the train steamed out. . . . Boys leant out of the carriage windows, grimacing and cheering. The master in charge leant out, shaking his fist and shouting reproaches that were carried away by the wind. William and Ginger made a dash at the last carriage and were dragged from it by the porter with such violence that they both sat down hard and heavily upon the platform.

"Breakin' your necks and gettin' me into trouble!" said the porter angrily.

"I jolly well hope you *do* get into trouble," said

William, picking himself up and rubbing his bruises. "Stoppin' us like that when we're on work of nash'nal importance! You'd get into trouble all right if Mr. Churchill knew. I'd write to him about it if I'd got a stamp. What's goin' to happen to the food supply of the country with you goin' about knockin' everyone down what's tryin' to put it right? Serve you jolly well right if you had to starve."

"Aw, shut up," said the porter, losing interest in them and going to the ticket collector's office for his cup of tea.

William poked his head round the door.

"When's the nex' train?" he said.

The porter, his mouth full of elevenses, made a threatening gesture.

"Eleven five," said the ticket collector shortly. "And get out! We've had enough of you."

"An' *we've* had *more'n* enough of you," said William, discreetly taking to his heels as he said it.

Realising that the ticket collector was not pursuing them, they paused for breath at the end of the road.

"Well, that gives us about twenty minutes," said William, looking at the church clock. "What'll we do with it?"

"We'd better not miss the nex' one," said Ginger uneasily.

"No, we won't miss the nex' one," William assured him. "I bet they won't have done much by the time we get there, either. I bet they won't even have started. I bet it's a good thing to come by a later train really. . . . Let's have a climb of that tree in Jenks' field. We'll start diff'rent sides an' race up it."

"BREAKIN' YOUR NECKS AND GETTIN' ME INTO TROUBLE,"
SAID THE PORTER ANGRILY.

They started the race, met half-way, fought for the same foothold, lost their balance and fell to the ground, rolling into the ditch that bordered the field.

"That's a draw, too," said William, picking himself up from the ditch and removing a few weeds from his mouth. "And you've got another tear in your jersey."

"So've you," retorted Ginger.

The church clock struck eleven.

"Come on. We've got to catch that train."

They caught the train, even finding time for an exchange of hostilities with the porter before it came in Immediately it came in, the porter opened a carriage door, picked them up, one after the other, and threw them on to the floor of the carriage.

"Good riddance!" he said.

"Same here," shouted William from the carriage window as the train began to move off

Ginger, scrambling to his feet, pushed William aside and leant out of the carriage window in his turn.

"Bats!" he shouted to the porter, touching his head.

"Thought so, poor chaps!" said the porter, deliberately misunderstanding him.

Satisfied, on the whole, with their conduct of the feud, the two started scuffling about the empty carriage, pushing each other on to the floor, trying to force each other under the seats. . . . The quarter of an hour or so between the two stations was pleasantly passed in this way, though at the end their features were almost indiscernible beneath the additional coating of grime that the process had imparted to them.

"Gosh! You do look a sight," said Ginger, as they tumbled together out of the carriage on to the tiny station of Applelea.

"I couldn't look worse than you," retorted William with spirit.

"Well, it doesn't matter, anyway," said Ginger philosophically. "We're only goin' fruit-pickin'. They said come in ole clothes."

"Well, they look that all right by now," said William. "Come on. Let's start for this farm. . . . *Gosh!*"

They stared at each other in consternation, realising that neither of them knew where the farm was.

"Fancy you not findin' *that* out," said William severely.

"Fancy *you* not! Thought you were so clever."

They wrangled amicably on these lines for a few minutes, then William said:

"Well, I bet we find it all right. It can't be far off in a little place like this. I know it's up a hill, 'cause ole Markie said it would be a hard day's work for us an' there was a walk up a hill before we got to this farm, so we mustn't tire ourselves out before we started. . . . Come on! Let's find a hill. I bet we get there before they've done anythin'."

"There's a hill jus' outside the station. That'll be the one."

They set off briskly up the hill. At the top stood a solitary house, after which the road seemed to degenerate into a cart track descending into the valley below. William and Ginger stood looking at the house.

"It isn't a farm at all,'¹ said William. "It's called Cray House."

"An' I don't see any boys about," said Ginger, peering through the hedge. "I don't see anyone at all. . . ."

"P'raps they're on the other side of the house."

"We'd hear 'em if they were."

"Well, let's go'n' have a look round, now we're here. They may be workin' so hard they've no time to talk."

They entered by the side gate and made their way across the lawn to a kitchen garden.

"Gooseberries!" said Ginger.

There they were—bushes of gooseberries, laden with fruit ready for picking.

"Gosh! It's time someone started on 'em."

"Well, I bet it'd help to solve the nation's food problems more if we picked these than if we went on climbin' hills for nothin' all mornin'. Everyone wants their fruit picked. Stands to reason. Let's start on it."

"We'd better ask first," said Ginger.

"All right," said William. "I'll go 'n' ask 'em. I bet they'll be jolly grateful. Shouldn't be surprised if they gave us some to take home."

He went up to the front door and knocked boldly. No one answered. He went round the house and knocked, more boldly, at the back door. Still no one answered. Growing yet bolder, he peered in at all the downstairs windows, then returned to Ginger.

"No one's in," he said. He looked thoughtfully at the laden gooseberry bushes. "Well, I'm goin' to start on 'em. I'd made up my mind to spend to-day solvin' the nation's food problem an' I'm not goin' to waste it, wanderin' about an' climbin' hills, lookin' for the others. There may be hundreds of hills. . . . We could spend all day goin' up an' down 'em. . . . Come on. Let's start."

They worked hard—seldom speaking, not eating a single gooseberry—till the clock struck one.

"They'll have come in for lunch now," said William. "I'll go 'n' tell 'em what we've done. They'll be jolly pleased."

He went up to the house again, knocked at all the doors, looked in at all the windows and returned to Ginger.

"They're still out," he said. "If they don't come back before we go, we'll leave the baskets on the front doorstep for them to find when they come home. They won't know who's done it, but I bet they'll be jolly pleased. Let's have our lunch now."

Sitting on the ground among the bushes, they ate their sandwiches, still abstaining with conscious effort from the tempting fruit.

"I bet we've done enough pickin'," said William, as he swallowed his last mouthful of (powdered) egg sandwich. "I'm scratched all over an' my back's nearly cracked across the middle with bendin' an' I'm gettin' so thirsty that, if I go on much longer, I shall start eatin' 'em. Let's jus' pick six more each an' then take 'em round to the house an' go home."

They picked six more each, then stood upright, stretching their aching limbs.

"Gosh, I'm stiff," said William. Suddenly he stopped motionless, staring at the drive. "Look!" he whispered.

A woman, carrying a shopping basket, was walking

up the drive to the front door. At the front door she put down the basket and took a latch-key from her coat pocket.

"Come on," said William.

The woman, having opened the door, turned to see two boys standing just behind her, each holding a basket of gooseberries.

"LOOK," SAID WILLIAM, STARING AT THE DRIVE.

We've picked your gooseberries," said William.

"Oh, yes," said the woman unconcernedly, as if it were quite a usual proceeding. "That's all right."

"What shall we do with them?" said William, a little taken aback by her attitude

"You'd better take them, I suppose," said the woman, as if she had no further interest in the matter.

"T-t-t-take them?" stammered William in surprise.

"Of course," laughed the woman. She had a pleasant good-tempered laugh.

"D-d-don't you want 'em?"

"It doesn't matter whether I want them or not, does it?" she said. "You've come and picked them and you must take them. Have you had something to eat, by the way?"

William was too much bewildered to reply, but Ginger managed to stammer out, "Y-yes, thanks, we brought sandwiches."

"That's all right," said the woman. "And now, off with you! I've got all my housework to do."

She went in and closed the door. William and Ginger were left, holding their baskets of gooseberries and gaping at each other.

"What are we goin' to do?" said Ginger. "I don't think we ought to take 'em."

"She said we could," said William. "She's *giv'n* them to us. She mus' be jolly kind. Or p'raps she doesn't like gooseberries. I'm jolly well goin' to take mine, anyway."

"All right. I'm goin' to take mine, too."

"An' let's go quick before she changes her mind."

They walked down the hill to the station, tired but happy, eating gooseberries as they went.

"They're jolly good," said William. "They're the best I've ever tasted. Well, it helps to solve the nation's food problem, anyway, 'cause I bet I shan't want any tea after this."

"One always feels like that when one's eatin' things," said Ginger, "but, when tea time comes, one feels diff'rent."

"Yes," agreed William, "I've noticed that, too. You seem to have a sep'rate appetite for meals. . . . I don't think I can eat all these. I think I'll give 'em to my mother an' she can make somethin' of them. That'll help solve the nation's food problem all right."

Mrs. Brown, presented with the gooseberries, was touched and relieved.

"Well, William, it shows you worked really hard. I was so afraid you'd get into some sort of mischief." She looked at the basket with increasing surprise. "You mean they gave you all these?"

"Yes."

"I suppose they had more than they wanted. It was very kind of them and it shows you worked well. . . . Did you enjoy the day?"

"Yes, thanks," said William, deciding that it would serve no useful purpose to describe the various complications the day had offered.

"You look perfectly frightful, of course, but I suppose that's only natural. You'd better go and have a bath. The water's nice and hot." She looked at the gooseberries again. "Actually I've no more sugar for jam, and I've bottled as many as I can spare bottles for. . . ." An idea suddenly struck her. "I tell you what! I'll raffle them at the Red Cross Sale to-morrow. You can take them round for me. You said you'd come and help me, you know. I believe there's a prize for the one who sells the most raffle tickets, so you may win that. . . .   Anyway, it's a very useful war effort, dear, and you ought to help."

"All right," sighed William.

Then a thoughtful look came into his face. He had remembered suddenly that the basket had been "borrowed" from Mrs. Bott. Oh well, he consoled himself, all baskets look alike and I'll take it back as soon as the Sale's over. . . .

Spruce, clean, his hair sleeked back from his frowning brow, wearing best suit, spotless collar, immaculate tie, William wandered to and fro in the crowded hall, carrying his basket of gooseberries and his raffle tickets. . . . Suddenly he noticed his mother talking to the woman who had given him the gooseberries. Not knowing whether she would like to see her gift thus exposed for sale, he was on the point of quietly merging with the crowd when his mother called him.

"Come here, William. Let Mrs. Hallowes buy a ticket for the raffle."

Mrs. Hallowes looked at William, obviously without recognising him, then transferred her attention to the gooseberries. "Yes, I will have a ticket, please. They look delicious—rather like those in my own garden, of which I've not been allowed *one*."

"Haven't you really?" said Mrs. Brown.

"No. The house belongs to the Botts, you know, and when we took it, just for the summer, they said that we couldn't have the fruit, as it had all been sold to Netherby's in Hadley. I adore gooseberries, and it's been terribly tantalising to watch them ripen and

not to be able even to taste them. . . . I was quite
relieved when Netherby's started to pick them yesterday. They sent two of the most filthy ragged
little urchins you ever saw. Fruit-pickers, I suppose,
from the East End. I went round the garden after-
wards to make sure that they'd taken nothing else,
but they seemed only to have taken the gooseberries. . . .
Is this your little boy?"

"Yes, this is William. . . . Say 'how d'you do' to
Mrs. Hallowes, William."

William fixed a glassy smile on Mrs. Hallowes and
said: "How d'you do."

She looked at him in a puzzled way.

"How very odd!" she said, then laughed as she
turned to Mrs. Brown. "I mean, it's odd how all boys
of that age seem to resemble each other." She looked
again at William. "Yes, dear, I'd like one of the
tickets. I'm *very* fond of gooseberries."

She bought a ticket, and William moved off to join
Ginger at the further end of the hall. Ginger was
wandering about disconsolately with a tray of "but-
tonholes" that had been hastily and not very artistic-
ally put together by Mrs. Monks the evening before.
Both trade and blooms were flagging considerably.

"I say!" said William. "Those gooseberries we
got yesterday. . . . They're sold an' Netherby's bought
'em an' she thought we were pickin' 'em for Netherby's.
No wonder she let us take 'em. They're Mrs. Bott's
really, 'cause the house belongs to Mrs. Bott. An'
she's here an' Mr. Netherby's here an' I've jus' heard
someone say that Mrs. Bott's comin' an' this is Mrs.
Bott's basket. What are we goin' to do?"

"*Gosh!*" said Ginger, aghast. "Where is she?"

"Over there, talkin' to my mother," said William.

They peered through the crowd and again met the lady's eye. She looked from William to Ginger, from Ginger to William, from William to the basket of gooseberries, and a startled look came into her face.

"Come on!" said William. "Let's get somewhere where she can't see us and keep well out of their way. It might be all right. . . ."

But William and his gooseberries were popular, and it was difficult to escape attention. His only rivals in the raffles line were a tea cosy and a magenta scarf, both wearing a war-weary air. His tickets melted like snow. . . . He had reached the last page of them when Mrs. Bott arrived. She looked hot and angry. Mr. Netherby, small and stout and shining, Hadley's leading fruiterer and, this year, its mayor, received her.

"Sorry I'm late," she said. "Lorst me clothes coopongs. Been hunting for them all morning. Can't find 'em anywhere. Stole off me, I shouldn't be surprised—an' not likely to get 'em replaced, not if I know this 'ere government. In rags, I am. Hardly a stitch to me back. I could have cried me eyes out, I was that upset. I nearly sent to say I couldn't come. . . ."

"I'll do what I can for you, of course, Mrs. Bott, in my official capacity," said Mr. Netherby.

"Thanks," said Mrs. Bott ungraciously. "That's not likely to be much."

Mrs. Bott was annoyed that Mr. Netherby had been asked to open the bazaar instead of herself. She considered that opening bazaars in the neighbourhood was her prerogative. In spite of this, however, she was prepared to act handsomely, and she went round the stalls, flinging pound notes carelessly to left and right, telling over and over again the story of the lost clothing coupons.

"I've no 'eart for this sort of thing really," she said to Mrs. Monks, who sat behind a stall of drooping vegetation (for it had been collected the night before and the day had been a hot one). "Not when I think of myself goin' about for the next six months with me clothes droppin' off me back." At this point she saw William skulking in the background with his basket of gooseberries. "Here, you, William Brown! What mischief are you up to now?"

William stepped forward reluctantly, trying to shield the basket from its owner's view. But it was the gooseberries at which the lady was gazing.

"Where did you get them gooseberries?" she said sharply.

"I'm rafflin' them," said William.

"Where did you get 'em, I said."

"They were a present to my mother," said William, trying to speak with dignity and assuming his most wooden expression.

"Oh," said Mrs. Bott. "I'll take a ticket. They're like the ones at Cray House. I've sold them to Netherby's but I've regretted it ever since. They're a sight better than any we have at the Hall. I wish I'd kept 'em. How much?"

"Sixpence," said William.

Mrs. Bott handed him sixpence and took her ticket.

Mr. Netherby came up to them, rubbing his hands together.

"WHERE DID YOU GET THEM GOOSEBERRIES?" SAID
MRS. BOTT SHARPLY.

"What's all this? What's all this?" he said play-
fully. "Gooseberries?"

"This boy's raffling 'em," said Mrs. Bott shortly.
"I'm just saying that they're like the ones at Cray
House. I wish I hadn't sold you them now. I went

past the place this morning and saw you'd started picking 'em."

"Cray House?" said Mr. Netherby thoughtfully. "No, we've done no picking at Cray House yet."

Mrs. Bott stared at him.

"No picking at Cray House? Why, all them bushes near the road was *stripped*."

"Not by us," said Mr. Netherby firmly. "We were going to start next week."

The colour suffused Mrs. Bott's flabby cheeks.

"Well, of all the——! And I told 'er plain as plain that she wasn't to touch 'em. It's wrote down in black an' white in the agreement. Robbery, that's what it is! Sheer robbery! Wore out as I am with worry over this 'ere clothes coopong business, I'll go and see my solicitor first thing in the morning. She can't get away with a trick like that, not with me. I'll make her pay for it, all right."

Mrs. Bott's nostrils were dilated with anger. Her snort was the snort of an enraged war horse. At that moment, Mrs. Hallowes, placid and smiling, approached her.

"Good afternoon, Mrs. Bott," she said pleasantly. "I must pay my respects to my landlady."

Mrs. Bott breathed heavily.

"About them gooseberries, Mrs. Hallowes," she said.

"Oh, yes. Mr. Netherby's started picking them," said Mrs. Hallowes.

"I've just told Mrs. Bott," said Mr. Netherby gently, "that I haven't sent anyone to pick at Cray House yet."

"But you sent two boys. They came yesterday. They spent all morning picking and took the gooseberries away with them."

"You say that two boys came and said they were from Netherby's and picked my gooseberries?" said Mrs. Bott with ominous quiet.

"Yes," said Mrs. Hallowes. "At least, I understood that they were from Netherby's. They certainly picked the fruit and took it away with them."

"What were they like?"

"Filthy ragged little urchins. I took it for granted that they were children from the East End of London who'd come out into the country for the fruit picking. . . . And yet—it's odd," she added thoughtfully.

"What's odd?" snapped Mrs. Bott.

"There are two boys here who are extraordinarily like them. They can't be the same ones, of course, because these are quite well-dressed and clean, but— they *are* extraordinarily like those two little urchins."

"Show me them boys," said Mrs. Bott between her teeth.

But William and Ginger had not waited for the end of the conversation. Quietly, unobtrusively, unperceived by the busy crowd around them, they had taken refuge beneath the nearest stall, and Mrs. Hallowes' search was vain.

Mr. Netherby was ushering a select party on to the platform for the awarding of the prizes. There was Mrs. Bott, who always had to be on the platform or know the reason why; Mrs. Hallowes, who had won the basket of gooseberries; two nondescript ladies, who had won the tea cosy and the magenta scarf; and Mrs. Brown, for no other reason than that there was a chair to spare and her stall was nearest the platform. William had by now been indignantly ejected by the owner of the stall under which he had taken refuge, and was standing at the back of the hall, trying to conceal himself behind a woman in a broad-brimmed home-made raffia hat.

Mr. Netherby, who much enjoyed the sound of his own voice, opened proceedings by a long discourse on the aims and achievements of the Red Cross, occasionally directing reproachful glances at Mrs. Bott, who was keeping up a whispered conversation with Mrs. Hallowes across the table behind which he stood.

"What time did them boys come to you?"

"They were there when I got back from shopping. I'd had lunch in Hadley. It was about two."

"Where are them boys that you said were like them? Can you see 'em now?"

"Ladies, ladies!" said Mr. Netherby, looking up despairingly from his notes.

"Can you see 'em now?" repeated Mrs. Bott, raising her voice and glaring defiantly at Mr. Netherby.

At that moment the woman with the raffia hat stepped aside, and William was exposed to the full view of the platform.

"That's one of them," said Mrs. Hallowes, pointing him out to Mrs. Bott.

"William Brown!" said Mrs. Bott grimly. "I might have known!" She leant still further over Mr. Netherby and accosted Mrs. Brown.

"Mrs. Brown!"

"Yes," said Mrs. Brown, startled.

"This splendid movement has now reached such proportions," fairly shouted Mr. Netherby in an attempt to divert the attention of his audience from the vagaries of his platform colleagues.

"Are you aware that your William spent all yesterday morning stealing my gooseberries?"

"He did no such thing," said Mrs. Brown indignantly. "He was at Applelea all yesterday morning fruit picking."

"Reached such proportions . . ." repeated Mr. Netherby still more loudly, fixing a stern eye on Mrs. Brown.

"That's what I'm telling you. He was at Applelea, all right, on my property stealing of my gooseberries."

"I will now give you a few figures to show the immensity of this work," said Mr. Netherby, throwing an appealing glance at Mrs. Monks and silently imploring her to take control of the situation. There were, indeed, few situations beyond Mrs. Monks' control, but just now she was, like the rest of the audience, so taken up with trying to hear what Mrs. Bott and Mrs. Brown were saying that she had no attention to spare for Mr. Netherby.

"You're quite mistaken, Mrs. Bott," said Mrs. Brown with spirit. "He was with his school and in charge of one of his schoolmasters picking fruit at a farm."

"Where did he get them gooseberries, then?"

"They were a present to him."

Mrs. Bott snorted so loudly that Mr Netherby, surrendering to Fate, decided to cut the rest of his speech and get down to business.

"The prize for selling the greatest number of raffle tickets goes to William Brown," he said, "who has been raffling a basket of gooseberries." Another snort from Mrs. Bott drowned the end of his sentence, but he continued manfully, "Mrs. Hallowes is the winner of the basket of gooseberries. William Brown, will you come up and present your basket of gooseberries to Mrs. Hallowes? After which Mrs. Bott will present you with your prize."

"I will an' all," said Mrs. Bott, her voice tremulous with rage. "I'll give 'im 'is prize all right when he gets 'ere."

"You'll make a little speech about it, won't you, Mrs. Bott?" said Mr. Netherby officiously.

"I'll make a little speech, all right," said Mrs. Bott with lips grimly set.

"Will you come up to the platform, William Brown?" said Mr. Netherby.

William found himself being propelled by well-meaning hands towards the platform. His struggles to escape were looked upon as natural if uncharacteristic modesty.

"He's shy, poor little soul," murmured the woman in the raffia hat, who was a newcomer to the district.

Willy-nilly, William was forced to advance towards the array of hostile forces on the platform—Mrs. Bott, her face still purple with anger, Mr. Netherby, looking stern and startled (for Mrs. Bott had just whispered, "That's the boy what done it"), Mrs. Hallowes, looking sorrowful and shocked, Mrs. Brown, bewildered and apprehensive. At the bottom of the steps he stopped and made a last despairing effort to escape back into the hall, but the well-meaning hands still urged him up the steps. And on the top one he stumbled. . . . The basket fell from his hands, gooseberries rolled all over the floor, the piece of newspaper came out of the bottom of the basket, and from under the newspaper a little pink paper booklet fell at Mrs. Bott's feet.

"Me clothes coopongs!" she screamed, pouncing upon it eagerly, her eyes shining with joy, her whole face radiant. "Oh, me clothes coopongs! An' I thought I'd never see 'em no more."

"What *is* happening?" said Mrs. Brown despairingly.

"I remember now," said Mrs. Bott, almost hysterical with delight. "It was on Friday. I'd started off shopping and forgot me basket, so I popped into the shed for me gardening basket to save me going back to the house and I popped me clothes coopongs under the bit of newspaper at the bottom to keep 'em safe. And I quite forgot I'd done it and I'd never have remembered till kingdom come if it hadn't been for this boy. Never. I've got a memory like a sieve. And I don't allow no one else to use this gardening basket. I keep it for me own gardening, and, to tell the truth, I don't do much. I ain't got the figure for it. They'd have stayed in that there basket for months, with me goin' about in rags. . . ."

"But what about the gooseberries?" said Mr. Netherby with a sternly judicial air. "Did or did not this boy take them from Mrs. Hallowes' garden?"

"You leave this boy alone," said Mrs. Bott, drawing William's unwilling head to her breast and impaling it on a diamond brooch. "He's found me clothes coopongs for me, which is more'n you ever did, and I shall be grateful to him the rest of me life. He's welcome to all the gooseberries I've got an' more. You come round to the Hall to-morrow, ducks, and take all the gooseberries you want. You can 'ave a peach or two, too, if you like. I'll never forget what you've done for me to-day. Never all me life."

"Well, hadn't we better get on with proceedings?"

said Mr. Netherby, piqued by Mrs. Bott's sudden change of front and realising that the audience was growing restive. "Perhaps someone will kindly pick up the gooseberries, and then perhaps Mrs. Bott will kindly present the prize to William Brown."

A dozen children ran up to the platform to retrieve the gooseberries. Mr. Netherby strode about directing them and crushing gooseberries into the floor at every step. The children returned to their seats,

"YOU LEAVE THIS BOY ALONE!"   MRS. BOTT IMPALED
WILLIAM'S HEAD ON A DIAMOND BROOCH.

munching happily. A few of the gooseberries had found their way back into the basket and these William presented solemnly to Mrs. Hallowes. . . . Then Mrs. Bott, still beaming happily, clasping her book of clothes coupons in both hands, rose to make her speech. It was a rambling incoherent speech. No one was quite sure what William was getting his prize for, except that it was for some act of heroism out of the common. One or two had a vague idea that he had

saved Mrs. Bott's life and was being presented with one of the Humane Society's medals. . . . Actually the prize was a bar of chocolate to which Mrs. Bott impulsively added half a crown.

"And I wish there was more boys like you, William," she said earnestly. "I've misjudged you in the past, but I won't never do so no more. Me in all that trouble and all these people just sitting about and not raisin' a finger to 'elp me, and you going quietly off like that to find me clothes coopongs. . . ."

It was evident that, so great was her joy and relief, she was a little vague as to the exact circumstances in which her lost coupons had been found. But she knew that they had been found and brought to her by William . . . and she still beamed on him tenderly as he made his way with his mother across the crowded hall. . . .

"And now, William, please tell me what all this was about," said Mrs. Brown, as soon as they were outside the hall and on their way home. "Whose *were* the gooseberries?"

"Well, it *is* a bit confusing," admitted William, "but the way it happened was this . . ."

THE END